To the Pennington
family—

THAIRYN
and the
THIEVES

Remember
it's what's inside
that counts!
Yours in writing—
Nan Whybark

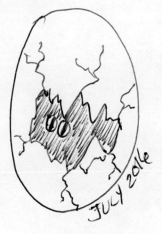

JULY 2016

THAIRYN
and the
THIEVES

Book 4
Earth to Irth Series

NAN WHYBARK

THAIRYN AND THE THIEVES
BOOK 4

iUniverse books may be ordered through booksellers or by contacting:

iUniverse
1663 Liberty Drive
Bloomington, IN 47403
www.iuniverse.com
1-800-Authors (1-800-288-4677)

ISBN: 978-1-4917-9720-4 (sc)
ISBN: 978-1-4917-9721-1 (e)

Library of Congress Control Number: 2016907858

Print information available on the last page.

iUniverse rev. date: 05/27/2016

Also by Nan Whybark

The Weasel and the Wizard: Earth to Irth Series, Book 1

The Serpent and the Sorceress: Earth to Irth Series, Book 2

The Matriarch and the Magic: Earth to Irth Series, Book 3

Dedicated with love and gratitude
to my father,
Nathan Jack Newby,
who always has a mischievous twinkle in his eye;
who inspired my first writings and drawings,
and taught me about wonderful creatures and daring adventure.

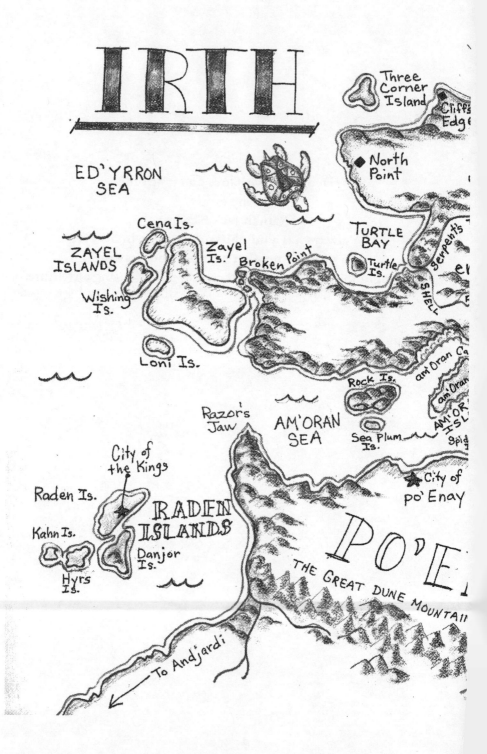

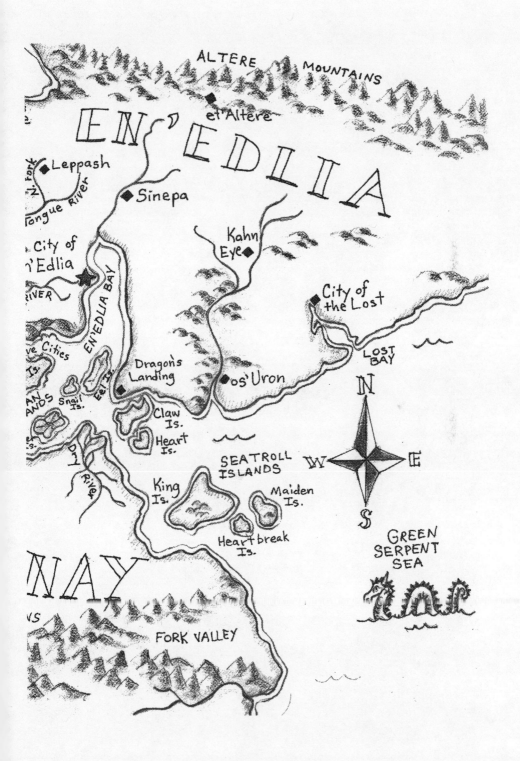

IRTH'S GLOSSARY
FOR OFF-WORLDERS

am'Oran: A large series of underwater caves that form the communities of this city populated by the am'Orans.

am'Orans: A race of gentle humanoids who are child-like in their appearance with pale, blue skin, large dark-blue eyes and white hair. They live in underwater cave communities. They have gill vents on their necks for underwater breathing, and also lungs to breathe air. They have established trade with land dwellers on Irth. Their trade items include fossi-shells, delicate deep-sea fish, singing sea turtles and other rarities from the sea.

am'Oranth: The early rising first moon of Irth. It has a soft pearly-white luster that is dim, yet beautiful. It is said that the am'Oran people were named for this moon due to their pale, luminous complexions (Also see ul'Daman, Irth's other moon).

AquaVelvet Fish: a blue-green fish that has velvety skin highly prized for making exotic hats and bags. Also good to eat with squirting sea plums and muffybread.

Birth-gift: A magical ability that in inherited at birth by those of Irth. The gift is not evident at first, but usually surfaces in children by the age of five. The children must then learn to use, control and strengthen their gift as they grow to maturity. Parents and schools help in this process. Some gifts may determine future jobs or duties.

Bloat Fish: smallish, tan colored fish that has an inner sac it inflates with air to make itself too large to be swallowed by an attacking predator. (Also see "Waterblimp").

Bottom Spider: An eight-legged crustacean about eight inches long with two body parts. They are edible, although their meat is very salty and mushy. They are helpful in cleaning up debris on the sea floor. They are food for many types of fish and other creatures.

Breakfast bug: A tiny insect that often flies blindly into spider webs, containers of food or drink in the early light of morning. Hence, it is often eaten for breakfast intentionally or accidentally. High in protein and other nutrients, it is largely ignored or even considered good fortune when found in something about to be eaten. Also used as a derogatory name for someone with little sense.

Bumphead: a pasture animal the size of a miniature horse. It has long, shaggy hair, horns that grow up and back from the shoulders, and dark pink eyes with triangular pupils. It is usually a gentle animal, but during mating season the male becomes violent, ramming into other males with its head. This ramming behavior often creates permanent lumps on the head. The bumpier the head, the stronger the animal. It is bred primarily in Leppash and highly prized for the female's sweetwater (see Sweetwater), horns- used in making tools and instruments- and hair- used in creating yarn for weaving fabrics. Its hair is silky soft and usually off white or, very rarely, emerald-green. These rarities are reserved only for the patriarchal family and the extremely wealthy. They are considered good luck and are never killed for meat or sport, but their hair is sheared and sold yearly. Also used as a derogatory name among males for someone who is easily riled up.

City Council Representative: A member of the High council, this person's main duty is to represent the voice of the common people of en'Edlia on matters discussed at council meetings. He must be impartial to his own desires and vote as the majority of the people dictate. He also brings to the council items of concern brought up in City Council meetings, and then returns the High council decisions or suggestions on those matters to the City Council. Birth-gifts that help in this position are all-hearing ears and mental-audio memory. Currently Patriarch Pepperton holds this position.

Cloud fruit: A large, white, tree fruit that resembles the shape of a cloud. It has pale blue seeds and white, spongy, yet juicy, insides. The outer skin is smooth and ranges in color from white to dark gray as it ripens. Left to rot on the tree, the fruit will drop its seeds to the ground, and then dry up and blow away. This fruit is best when eaten fresh.

Crown Matriarch: If there is no son born to the high patriarchal family, the eldest daughter becomes Crown Matriarch at her father's death. If the High Matriarch is still living, she and the Crown Matriarch take on a co-leadership position until the High Matriarch's death. At that time, the Crown Matriarch becomes High Matriarch and her husband, if she has one, takes up the title of High Patriarch.

Crown Patriarch: The eldest son of a High Patriarch, who usually inherits the title of High Patriarch at his father's death. In some cases, as stated above (see Crown Matriarch), the husband of a Crown Matriarch would be considered Crown Patriarch until the High Matriarch's death. Then he would assume the position of High Patriarch.

Dark Magic: The evil side of magic, avoided by most on Irth, but embraced by those seeking power, riches or other undue glory and desiring to take it by force. Such was the magic of the Wizard Zarcon at the time Broktomerris, Merrick's father, was high patriarch in en'Edlia. (see Book 1- "The Weasel and the Wizard") and the Sorceress Odethia (see Book 2- "The Serpent and the Sorceress").

Dragon's Landing: An eastern seaside city in the country of en'Edlia (see map). A lesser trade port frequented by dragon riders, dragon raisers, dragon egg traders, and those with similar interests.

en'Edlia: The largest country on Irth, ruled by a patriarchal council system. It is a major seaport and trade center. The royal crest is a white and gold winged seashell on a field of emerald green. Current High Patriarch is Merrickobrokt, son of Broktomerris and Narrianamyesa.

et'Altere: A group of villages under one ruler, The Great Altere, in the Altere Mountains (see et'Alterens; Great Altere; also map)

et'Alterens: The people from the et'Altere villages who often dress in furs of animals for warmth. They are called et'Als as slang for et'Alterens by some people of larger cities and are somewhat looked down upon as less educated and cultured. This is not true, but a perceived notion due to the shy and reclusive nature of these people. (see et'Altere; Great Altere)

Firedrake: A dragon-like creature, about the size of a large falcon, used in hunting or sport. It can be trained to respond to whistles or other commands. It is fiercely loyal to its master and will die in protecting him or her. Cannot be bred in captivity. Must be captured in the wild.

Flying Catlin: A winged feline-type animal bred and raised in North Point, and trained to deliver messages. Most are black and white striped, from ears to tail, with blue-black feathered wings. Sworn to its duty as messenger, it can also be playful, aloof, annoying, proud and loveable. Not kept as a pet due to its flighty nature.

Foreign Trade Minister: A member of the High council, this person's main duty is to ensure that trade between other countries and en'Edlia is fairly priced, safe for the consumer, and delivered undamaged. He travels to other countries to set up trade agreements for both imported and exported products. He must be versed in foreign customs, languages, and policies. In times of war, this position can be hazardous. Birth-gifts that can aid in these duties are speaking languages, x-ray vision and photographic memory. Currently in this position is Matriarch Birkin.

Fossi-shell: Shells of the fossi-snail that produce a blue phosphorescent radiance that grows brighter the colder it gets. Though mainly used for lighting am'Oran underwater cave communities, they are also used as trade items, although not as effective out of the cold sea depths. (see also Fossi- snail; am'Oran; am'Orans)

Fossi-snail: A type of deep-sea snail that imbues its shell with phosphorescence. They are seeded and farmed by the am'Orans; also used as a protein-rich food. (see Fossi-shell)

Go-betweens: The interior corridors inside the walls between rooms that can only be entered through secret doorways known to the high patriarchal family and their protectors. Often there are also small, secret panels that can be moved to allow spying or safely peeking into a room while remaining unseen. These were created to give extra protection to the patriarchal family from interior threats, invasion, and also to provide faster means of travel between palace rooms when needed for safety or convenience.

Great Altere: The ruler of et'Alteren villages. Elected by the people, the Great Altere serves as ruler until death. Seen as both a spiritual and secular leader, he or she is treated with great respect and loyalty, and has power to make laws, perform marriages, bless crops and declare war, among many other things. (see et'Altere; et'Alterens)

High Commander: A member of the high council, this person's main duty is to recruit, train, maintain, and deploy armed forces in the sworn duty to provide protection and help to the people of en'Edlia and its surrounding area. This includes smaller cities that are not under protection from any other country. The palace and local guards are included in this commander's force as he works with the High Keeper of the Peace. He has the added responsibility to recruit, train, maintain and deploy companies of soldiers in times of war. The high commander will then act as high commander of the land forces under the high council's direction. There are several birth-gifts which can aid in this duty, including impervious skin, teleportation of large masses and strengthening others. This position is currently held by Patriarch Kitzer.

High council: The governing body of en'Edlia made up of twelve men and women including the high patriarch and high matriarch currently ruling. (see High council Members)

High council Members: This ruling body of 12 men and women of en'Edlia currently includes: <u>High Patriarch</u> Merrick, <u>High Matriarch</u> Narrian, <u>Oracle</u>- Pth. Ardloh, <u>High Mariner</u>- Pth. Cebton, <u>High Commander</u>-Pth. Kitzer, <u>Sea Merchant Council Rep.-</u> Pth. Royer, <u>Land Merchant Council Rep.</u>- Mth. Shappel, <u>City Council Rep.</u>- Pth. Pepperton, <u>Foreign Trade Minister</u>- Mth. Birkin, <u>High Keeper of the</u>

Peace- Pth. Degler, Portal Guard Commander- Pth. Olec, Scribe- Pth. Cilcom. (see each office individually for a description of position duties)

High Keeper of the Peace: A member of the en'Edlia high council, this person's main duty is to maintain a peaceful environment in and around the city of en'Edlia, but extends to the whole country as well. The position is currently held by Patriarch Degler, who works with the portal guards and high commander.

High Mariner: A member of the high council, this person's main duty is to ensure that all ships are seaworthy, all crews are well treated, and to report incidents of piracy, abuse of crew members, slavery or incompetency in an admiralty, captainship or any officers. He works with the sea merchant's council to insure safe and adequate seafaring provisions for both the ships and the crews. He has an inspection crew that assists him in his work. He has the added responsibility to recruit, train, maintain and deploy a fleet of ships with their crews in times of war. The high mariner will then act as high commander of the sea fleet under the high council's direction. Several birth-gifts can aid in this duty, such as control of water, teleportation of large masses and breathing underwater. This position is currently held by Patriarch Cebton.

High Matriarch: Female leader of the realm of en'Edlia on the planet Irth. A member of the high council and usually wife of the high patriarch. On some occasions the high patriarch will die and a new high patriarch will be chosen, usually eldest son from ruling family. In these situations, the high matriarch retains her title until her death, and the wife of the new high patriarch is given the temporary title of crown matriarch.

High Patriarch: The male leader of the realm of en'Edlia on the planet Irth. He is the head of the high council, the governing group of 12. His wife is usually the high matriarch except in certain situations. The title position is usually handed down from father to eldest son, except when there is no son born to the regal family. In that case, the eldest daughter becomes crown matriarch. In rare cases due to corruption, the people have cast out a high patriarch by majority vote, and chosen another to replace him. (see Crown Matriarch; High Matriarch).

Hordle: A long-legged gentle animal the size of a large horse, with short curly hair, long narrow head, floppy ears and a long, slender tail that ends in a puff of hair. Its large, round eyes change color with the weather. Its feet are thickly padded on the bottom and end in six toes. The hair can be a variety of colors, including white, tan, pale yellow, chocolate brown and black, but never more than one color on any single animal. Hordles were imported from Leppash to the capital city of en'Edlia for the patriarchal family, specifically to pull the patriarchal coach. There are only twelve in the palace stables currently, and all are white.

Itchy-fruit: A soft, deliciously sweet fruit that can be eaten dried, raw, cooked or made into sauce or juice. The fruit's hairy, pink and yellow striped skin produces an allergen that creates intense itching when rubbed on people's skin. Be careful to wear protection when handling the fresh fruit. Seek medical attention on contact.

Irth's moons: am'Oranth and ul'Damen (see each individual listing for details)

Irth Star: a nocturnal bird that glows a soft yellow-orange. It has a long forked tail and slender wings. Often in large flocks, they are a spectacular sight, like swirling lights or dancing stars in the night sky.

King of the Sea Trolls: A legendary creature famous in many Irth children's tales. He ruled the sea trolls who controlled the seas and captured unsuspecting Irthlings lost at sea. He was known for loving an en'Edlian maiden who, though she loved him, could never be happy under the sea, and he could not live with her on the land. His heart broke when she drowned trying to return to her family.

Land Merchants Council Representative: a member of the high council, this person's main duty is to represent all the merchants, shopkeepers, business owners and other entrepreneurs that do their business on land. Although some may import wares from overseas, they do not have ships or business involving exportation of merchandise overseas without having a representative on the sea merchant's council as well. They take the voice of the people to the high council. The land merchant's council works with the foreign trade minister and the sea merchant's council to insure fair trade. Patriarch Shappel currently holds this position.

Leppash: An inland city, with wide-spread rural communities on grassy plains and rolling hills. It is known for its magnificent animal breeding. Creatures like hordles, bumpheads, and mozers are highly prized and sought after on Irth (see Bumphead; Hordle; Mozer).

Matria: A slang form of the word matriarch used by children to lovingly address their mothers. (Pronounced **maw**-tree-a).

Matriarch: The title given to a female when she reaches adulthood, starts her own family through marriage, becomes a business woman, or owner of land or property. It is a common title like Mistress, Madam, or Lady, and not to be confused with the realm titles of *High Matriarch or Crown Matriarch*. (see High Matriarch; Crown Matriarch)

Mozer: A slow, gentle pasture dwelling animal raised primarily in Leppash. It is exported to other cities and countries for its meat, hide, and production of sweetwater. Though not rare, it is highly valued and usually not afforded by the poorer classes of people (see Sweetwater).

Muffyberries: Bright yellow berries that are poisonous to humanoids until cooked. Used in breads and other dishes to add a sweet and sour flavor. The main food source for muffybirds and other fowl. (see also Muffybirds; Muffybread)

Muffybird: A medium-sized bird that is a mass of tangled grey and brown feathers. With very short wings, beak, and tail, it is hard to tell which end is which, especially when flying. It has a haphazard flight pattern and usually lands in a heap in a muffyberry bush. Often seen in groups of three or four. (see also Muffyberries)

Muffybread: a dense, whole grain bread made with muffyberries, nuts and seeds. A favorite breakfast food in en'Edlia. (see also Muffyberries)

Off-worlder: Any being that is from another world outside the one you live on.

Oracle: Recognized as a spiritual leader and part of the High council of en'Edlia. The oracle can be male or female and receives the office through the birth-gift. Very few are born with a birth-gift powerful enough to become oracle. Only one at a time may hold the office, usually the one with the strongest gift. Oracles can see into the future and have visions of things to come. They are sometimes ignored or considered a bit crazy by more contemporary thinkers. The current oracle is Patriarch Ardloh. The current oracle in training is Emija.

os'Uron: A rough seaport city south of en'Edlia, usually avoided by most other than scoundrels, scallywags, pirates and cutthroats, or those looking for such characters.

Palm-bomb: A fist-sized black, tough-shelled fruit that is native to the tropical climates of Irth. The meat inside of the shell is pale pink, sweet and chewy, yet juicy, with a slight nutty flavor. The center is filled with a jelly that contains three large seeds. The seeds are poisonous and should not be eaten raw or cooked. The jelly is edible, though I would not recommend it. If struck by a palm-bomb falling from a tree, it could render one unconscious or worse.

Pa'trees: A form of monetary exchange, pa'trees are coins made of brass. Their worth varies from country to country, but they are accepted as legal tender for purchases and payments.

Patria: A slang form of the word patriarch used by children to lovingly address their fathers. (Pronounced **paw**-tree-a).

Patriarch: The title given to a male once he reaches adulthood and/or becomes a head of household, owner of a business, land or property. It is a common title like Sir, Mister, or Lord, and not to be confused with the realm title of *High Patriarch* (see High Patriarch; Crown Patriarch).

po'Enay: A desert country across the sea from en'Edlia. There is open, friendly trade between the countries of po'Enay and en'Edlia and a few other cities nearby. It is said that long, long ago a strange tall, black-skinned off-worlder came to en'Edlia, took a wife and left on a ship across the sea. It is believed that the po'Enayans are their descendants and so related to those of en'Edlia as well (see map).

po'Enayans: The tall, slender, dark-skinned people of po'Enay. They have over-sized pointed ears, musical voices, and startling yellow eyes. Little clothing is needed in their home country, but when visiting the cooler climates, they wear long, flowing robes in bright, patterned colors of red, orange, yellow and blue. It is said they bring the desert sun and warmth with them. They have long, broad feet which help them navigate the desert sands. They never wear shoes. Their hair is the same color as their skin— a warm, deep brown— and is worn very short for both males and females. Only the king and queen have long, plaited hair ornately wrapped around their heads and fastened with beautifully hand-carved ornaments of gold, shell and bone.

Portal Guard Commander: A member of the en'Edlia high council, this person's main duty is to maintain a watchful guard, open and close the off-world portals that allow beings on and off Irth. Usually this position is given to one whose birth-gift is the ability to open portals, but one must be proven loyal and trustworthy to obtain the office. With a company of men at his disposal, the commander must keep a constant vigil to protect the lives and safety of all of Irth. He also communicates and collaborates with the other portal guard commanders in all other parts of Irth. The current person in this position is Patriarch Olec.

Rainbow Eel: A slender, sinuous fish with flashing rainbow colors along its sides. These colors are sloughed into the water and left in a trail when it is frightened, thus confusing its would-be attacker. It is considered good fortune to swim through an eel's rainbow trail. These eels are considered a delicacy in en'Edlia. Unfortunately the eel's lovely colors vanish when it dies, so eel skins are worthless.

Ruglump: A domesticated, gentle animal with long, soft hair, floppy ears, and large brown eyes. They are plump and cozy, sleeping most of the time. They can occasionally be roused to action by the smell of food, and love to be petted and scratched all over. A favorite pet for young children, they come in varying sizes and colors, including purple. Also a demeaning name for someone who is lazy.

Scribe: A member of the en'Edlia high council whose position is to take accurate notes during all council meetings, note the names of those present, and report or read back all notes from previous meetings as needed. The scribe is also responsible for the care, keeping and copying of all notes, certificates of registered birth-gifts, patriarchal family genealogy, declarations, proclamations, laws and other official documents of the realm of en'Edlia. The scribe may have others who assist him that have the appropriate birth-gifts and are approved by the high council.

Sea Merchant Council Representative: A member of the en'Edlia high council, this person's duty is to represent all merchants whose business involves transporting products over the sea. They are to bring concerns, piracy or other breaches of law to the attention of the high council, whether it be by one of their own local council or one from a foreign trade country. The sea merchant's council works with the foreign trade minister and the land merchant's council to insure fair trade.

Sea Slugs: Related to the slime snail, and can be used in similar ways, however they are much smaller and their slime is not as effective for waterproofing; it is more difficult to handle them due to the lack of a shell. They are often used by children in practical jokes. (also see Slime Snail)

Seraph-spiders: Thumbnail-sized golden colored spiders with small, iridescent wings. They can't really fly, but use their wings to glide and guide when descending long distances while making a web. They spew sturdy, deep-purple webbing.

Shell Fish: Tiny, silver and pink fish that find safety and shelter from predators in abandoned shells.

Sinepa: An inland city northeast of the city of en'Edlia known for its exotic flower and plant production. It exports bulbs, starts, cuttings and whole plants to other cities on Irth. It also imports foreign flora for the patriarchal palace gardens, along with garden displays in other cities and countries. The Sinepa Scarlett Sconce was developed and named for this city (see Sinepa Scarlett Sconce).

Sinepa Scarlet Sconce: An intensely red, blooming plant developed in Sinepa. The leaves, stems and roots of this plant are scarlet red. The lantern-like flowers are pure white with red veins and have an iridescent glow at night or in a dark room. Often used along garden pathways or as part of a bouquet on a table during the evening meal.

Singing Sea Turtles: Gentle sea turtles that rarely grow larger than a soup bowl, but emit the most melodious sounds that prove quite soothing to humanoids. They are often kept as pets, especially in sick-care houses. *Caution- these turtles can be dangerous!* When surrounded by a pod of these turtles, people have been known to drown because they relax so much they fall asleep in the water. Never keep more than one or two in the same place if you want to do anything but sleep. They are herded and raised as trade items by the am'Oran people.

Skitters: Long-tailed, soft, furry animals that live in burrows in the foothills of the Altere Mountains. Their slender bodies, small rounded ears, large, black eyes and whiskered, blue noses make these creatures popular pets. They are energetic, yet easily tamed. They make soft, whirring noises when petted. Children carry them wrapped around their necks or over their shoulders. Skitters are favorite bedtime partners and outdoor companions. The et'Alterens capture and tame them for trade. However they can be pests when allowed to run free in cities.

Slappers: See Slapphierocious

Slapphierocious: Commonly called slappers, they are a biting, flying insect that is irritating but not harmful, unless one is swarmed by them. In that event, it is advisable seek medical attention. Their bite leaves a red swollen bump on the skin that itches mildly, unless you are allergic.

Slime snail: A giant sea snail that produces vast quantities of slimy substance when removed from the sea. Ship builders gather these snails to waterproof the hulls of the ships before they are put into the sea for the first time. The snails are not harmed in this process and are returned to the sea when the job is finished. The only downside of the process is that the snails produce soft squeaking sounds when removed from the sea. It was long thought they were suffering, but research has shown the sound is made due to the huge amounts of slime being excreted from their bodies. The sound of over a hundred slime snails at work can be overwhelming; hence the ship builders are required to plug their ears with cloth during this process. Related to sea slugs. (see Sea Slugs)

Spectar-cats: Compared to a leopard of Earth, the spectar-cat is twice the size. These large animals have sleek, speckled coats of black, cream and orange. Green eyes are most common. Though generally gentle in natural, they can be deadly if provoked. They are native to the Raden Islands and some areas of po'Enay. Spectars are bred on the islands to serve and to protect the royal family. Two spectars can pull a cart with four grown people easily at about 25-30 miles-an-hour for about an hour without rest. There are also annual spectar-cat cart races that are highly competitive. These races are always won by the king of Raden, whether he deserves it or not.

Squirting Sea Plums: An underwater fruit that grows wild in many places. It is a lovely deep reddish-purple color with a salty skin and sweet, fruity flesh. The plants will squirt a deep purple liquid when disturbed. After harvesting, the fruit will squirt its seeds out when firmly pinched. It is delicious raw, dried or cooked. Sea plum juice is an excellent thirst quencher. It has become one of the intentionally planted and harvested sea crops produced by the am'Orans and traded with others on Irth (see am'Orans).

Sweetwater: A watery, pale-blue liquid produced by some female pasture animals, like the bumphead and the mozer. Used to nurse their young, it is also gathered and made into tasty curds that are exported to other cities on Irth. Sweetwater can be a refreshing drink on its own or flavored with other fruit or vegetable juices. (see Bumphead; Mozer)

ul'Damen: The late rising second moon of Irth. It is the brighter of the two. When full, it shines a gloriously brilliant orange-pink color. When setting, it deepens to a rusty-red. Some call ul'Damen the moon of love because of its warm color and late rising (see also am'Oranth, Irth's other moon).

Waterblimp: The hollow husk of the bloat fish that, when dried and then filled with water, becomes an excellent, easily breakable bomb for dousing unsuspecting victims. *Caution: Use at your own risk!* (see Bloat fish)

Xens: People of Irth that fear or are suspicious of off-worlders, especially in the ruling class. They have created a civil uprising and recruit those especially with dark magics. Their headquarters is in the Shards in the city of en'Edlia.

Zippers: See Zipperzuli-benefactus

Zipperzuli-benefactus: Commonly known as zippers, they are small, neon-blue flying insects that help pollinate plant life on Irth. Extremely fast moving. Tremendous wing-speed produces a buzzing sound. They produce zulijuice and are harmless to other creatures. (see Zulijuice)

Zulijuice: A thick, sweet liquid produced by the zipperzuli-benefactus. It is clear pale-purple in color, used in cooking and for sweetening drinks and other foods, and as food for other animals and insects, as well as a salve for healing burns. There are zulijuice farms on Irth, particularly in Leppash (see map).

Thairyn
hiding

CHAPTER 1

C rown Patriarch Thairyn raced around the lush, green bushes in the expansive palace gardens shouting and giggling. It was late afternoon, and he was having fun eluding his older twin sisters, Phyre and Jewl. In and out of the enchanting, yellow Krystin flowers he raced, and then around the Scarlet Sinepa Sconces, its red leaves fluttering and lantern-like blooms beginning to glow in the fading light. The sweet and spicy smell of the flowers swirled through the cooling air.

Thairyn slipped behind a garden bench into one of the carefully clipped hedges. He held his breath and tried hard not to laugh. He felt very clever. Playing catch-me-if-you-can was his favorite game.

Sometimes Father or Uncle Wayen would play. It wasn't very often, but those times were even more fun. They knew all the best places to hide while he was still learning. Yet at seven-going-on-eight years old, he felt he was quite an expert at this game already.

"I'm going to catch you, Thairyn!" yelled Jewl. He could hear her rustling dress and footsteps in the grass coming closer behind him.

"I'll find him first!" challenged Phyre. She ran right past her brother. Thairyn giggled.

Unfortunately, it was a little too loud. Phyre stopped and whirled toward the sound, her long copper-colored braid flying around. "I have you now," she whispered, holding her sunny-yellow dress still.

Holding his breath, Thairyn edged deeper into the shadowy hedgerow. Phyre was tiptoeing closer. Now he could see her smiling face, scanning the bushes with her sharp green eyes.

Closer . . . closer . . . closer Phyre came.

Suddenly, hands grabbed Thairyn from behind. Jewl's voice yelled, "Caught you!"

Startled, Thairyn let out a cry. A sharp branch scratched his face. "Ow!" he cried, tears springing up in his eyes as his sister dragged him backwards out of the hedge. He landed hard on the ground. His pride wounded more than his face.

"You hurt me, Jewl! I don't like you anymore. You're no fun to play with at all."

At that moment, red-haired Phyre came around the hedge. "Thairyn, you're bleeding!"

Jewl tucked her escaping dark-brown hair behind her ears and back into her long, single braid. "It's just a scratch," she said.

"It is not!" cried their brother. "It hurts, and I'll probably die now." Thairyn's slender body lay on the ground. His white and green tunic was grass stained, and his brown linen pants were dirty at the knees. He kicked out at Jewl, and then brushed the back of his hand over the scratch, smearing blood over his cheek.

"It wasn't my fault," Jewl barked.

"Now you're a mess," said Phyre as she looked at her brother's bloodied face and grass-stained clothes.

Jewl folded her arms, looking down at her brother. "Can't we just keep playing? It's almost time to go in." She brushed a leaf off the front of her long, sky-blue dress.

"I'm dying!" Thairyn shouted. "You don't even care!"

"You must be. I can smell you from here!" retorted Jewl.

"Come on, Thairyn. Let's play," coaxed Phyre. "Here, use this leaf to wipe your scratch. It will help it heal."

Jewl threw up her hands. "Well, I'm going to go do something else if Thairyn is going to act like a baby."

"I'm not a baby!" Thairyn yelled, pushing away the bruised leaf Phyre offered. "I'm the best catch-me-if-you-can player on Irth. That's my birth-gift!"

Jewl laughed, her bright-blue eyes flashing. "Then why did I find you?"

"Can't we just get back to the game?" Phyre held her hands out to both of her siblings.

"You know that's not your birth-gift, Thairyn," Jewl retorted. "You're like Phyre. Green-eyed and no birth-gift."

"Am not! Do too!" countered Thairyn. "Mother says just wait and it will come. You're just mean."

"It's all right if you don't have a birth-gift, Thairyn," Phyre soothed her brother while she kneeled trying to clean his face with the leaf. She turned a frowning glance up at Jewl. "Mother doesn't have one either."

"I don't care! It's not all right!" her brother yelled, pulling away. "I'm the crown patriarch, and I have a magic that nobody sees!"

"Here he goes again about his invisible powers. That's it. I'm going in!" Jewl turned toward the palace.

"Jewl, wait," Phyre begged.

"Well, I'm leaving too!" Thairyn cried and jumped up, his blond hair littered with leaves and twigs. "I'll show you! You'll never find me this time!" He ran deeper into the gardens as fast as he could away from his sisters. He'd show them, even if they were ten and he was only seven. His eyes blurred with tears of hurt and anger as he ran. He didn't care where he was going. He'd find a place they would never think to look.

"Thairyn! Come back!" shouted Phyre, quickly rising to her feet as she brushed off her yellow calf-length dress. "Jewl, help me!"

Jewl stopped, angrily turning around. "Why does he do this? He's just spoiled."

"Come on," Phyre pleaded. "We have to find him now. Father and Mother will be upset with us if we come back without him." She looked up at the darkening sky. "We'd better hurry."

Naron with the trunk

CHAPTER 2

Thairyn ran until he couldn't breathe anymore and his side burned like fire. He wiped his bloodied, sweaty face on the sleeve of his white tunic, and then he bent over with his hands on his knees, gasping for air. He had long since lost his anger, but the hurt of Jewl's words still stung like the scratch on his cheek. He wished now he had taken the leaf Phyre had offered him. It had smelled bitter, but she always knew what plants were good for this and that.

Looking around, Thairyn found himself in a part of the gardens he had never been in before. The plants here were wilder. There were no flowers either. The trees were taller, and the bushes rambled without any intentional paths or design. There was a rich smell of dirt and green leaves, mixed with the salty air from the nearby bay.

"This will be the perfect place to hide!" said Thairyn to himself. "I wonder if Uncle Wayen knows about this place." Thairyn wandered about aimlessly, tossing pebbles, looking for just the right spot to hide before his sisters caught up with him. *I'm such a fast runner, I have plenty of time,* he thought.

All at once, there was a huge man standing in front of him. The man wore big boots and a shabby, roughly woven jacket. He held a large, grubby linen bag, which smelled of dust and mold.

Alarmed, Thairyn looked up at the man's face. He thought he recognized the man, but his vision seemed blurry. He rubbed his eyes to clear them, and then looked again. *Oh, it's only Tesh, the gardener,* thought Thairyn with relief.

"Hello, Tesh," said Thairyn.

"Hello, young master," responded the man.

Thairyn wrinkled up his face. The voice was not Tesh's voice. It was too deep and rough.

"Are you sick, Tesh?" Thairyn said with concern. He stepped closer. "What are you doing way out here?"

"I'm looking for something," the man said, and he turned away.

Thairyn ran after the gardener then, eager to help him. "I'm good at finding things. Can I help you?"

"Yes, indeed!" rumbled the unfamiliar voice. "Let's look just around that tree." His large hand pointed to a huge trunk off to their left where the shadows deepened, and the brush was thick.

Thairyn smiled as he eagerly scampered toward the trunk. "What are we looking for?"

"Something small and helpless," the man said, taking two giant steps toward Thairyn's back. His lips parted in a frightening grin, showing discolored, crooked teeth.

Thairyn's head was down, scanning the bushes. "You mean like an animal?" he asked excitedly.

"No, I mean like YE!"

There was a sudden movement from behind the tree trunk, and another man lunged through the brush at the boy.

Thairyn's head snapped up, realizing too late that he was in danger. He tried to dash away, but the second man caught him by the arm and roughly yanked him back. Thairyn began to yell for help, but a filthy rag was stuffed into his mouth, while another rag was tied tightly around his head to hold the gag in place.

The would-be-gardener held him as well. Thairyn froze when he saw the big man's face blur and change. This was not Tesh. A great fear clutched at the boy's heart. He was in trouble. He wished he hadn't been so foolish. He wished he hadn't run away from Jewl and Phyre. He wished he had a magical power to turn himself into a dragon so he could protect himself. However, he knew his wishes wouldn't save him.

The huge man's face was very close now, unshaven and rough, with a big, fat, fleshy nose and small, squinty, dark eyes. Thairyn could smell his fishy breath as the man laughed in his face.

"I guess ye'll be coming with us now, won't ye!" sneered the second, smaller man.

"I just love catch-me-if-ye-can," murmured the big man.

Thairyn screamed through the rag. He pushed his tongue against it and gagged at its dirty, greasy taste. He squirmed, kicked, and fought his attackers' hold on him. Their hands were strong, and they laughed at him with deep, mocking guffaws.

"Wiry little fellow, ain't he, Arth?" laughed the smaller man, who wore a striped shirt. He tied the boy's hands together with cords, and then Arth tied the boy's ankles. Then they lifted Thairyn off the ground.

"Time for bed!" announced Arth. He popped his bag over Thairyn's head. The two men upended the boy into the sack, securing it with a rope. Thairyn's head painfully hit the ground. The boy continued to fight and make noise, thrashing inside the bag. The bag shed clouds of dust as Thairyn fought inside it.

"None of that now!" the smaller man whispered harshly. Thairyn felt a kick delivered to his back. When the boy continued to call out and thrash, he was kicked again, harder. "I said, none of that!"

Thairyn felt the toe of the man's boot hit him with bruising force. He sucked in a breath at the pain, hot tears and dust burning his eyes. He sneezed and then coughed. He was more hurt and angry and frightened than he had ever been in his young life. *What are they going to do to me?*

"Ye'll be still or we'll beat ye until ye are! Ye got me, whelp?"

"Don't hurt him, Tindus," Arth warned his partner. "Naron don't want no damaged goods."

Then, Thairyn felt himself lifted and slung over the big man's back like a sack of itchy fruit. Thairyn was jostled, upside-down, thumping in the sack against the man's back as the two men broke into a run. The frightened boy nervously jerked about as they crashed through the brush.

The clomping sound of the men's boots changed from soft thudding to hard slapping. Thairyn recognized the sound of cobblestone under their feet. Another few minutes passed with little sound but breathing, and the men's fast-paced gait. Soon the rumble of waves on the shore began to be near and getting nearer. The squeak and creak of ships docked at the pier accompanied the sharp cry of a seabird, and then the angle of the road sloped downward.

We're going to the bay! They're going to throw me in the bay! Thairyn's thoughts raced ahead. *I am going to die! I have to get away!*

Thairyn began to struggle against the ropes on his wrists. He jerked and tugged with all his might. The cording bit into his skin, but still he tried to loosen its hold on him.

"Be still in there!" Arth whispered, shaking the bag up and down. The jostling shifted Thairyn's position. His neck bent uncomfortably until his chin touched his chest. He could barely breathe, but still he pulled at the cords ignoring the big man's warning.

By the time his kidnappers came to a stop, Thairyn could no longer see light coming through the sack. *It must be dark outside now,* he thought. Then he heard the two men's voices again, and someone else's too.

"We got the package," Tindus, the smaller man said.

"Any trouble?" the new man asked.

"Not much. Walked right into our hands, he did."

"Good. The ship sails as soon as we board."

"What about the guards, Naron?" Arth questioned the third man.

"Let me handle that. I brought our bags and the trunk. Dump him in there."

Thairyn felt himself lowered into a box, and then a top clunked down over him. A strong, musty odor added to the already powerful stench of the sack. Thairyn sneezed again. He hoped he wouldn't throw up with the nasty gag in his mouth. There was the rattle of metal on metal. Then a muffled voice said, "That should hold him for a while. Let's go."

7

Again, Thairyn was lifted up and carried, this time inside a trunk. He wasn't sure what was happening. He could hear clomping feet and muffled voices. He was too scared to move, fearing he would be thrown into the sea at any moment.

*   *   *

"Your papers, sirs!" The uniformed dock guard stopped the three rough looking men carrying a trunk.

The men each pulled a rumpled paper from their clothes and handed them to the guard. Naron used his birth-gift to give the guard a sense of calm and peace. He could make people feel like everything was safe and secure while he robbed their pockets in plain sight.

"Seem to be in order," mumbled the guard. "What's in the trunk?"

"Just me personal possessions, sir," stated Arth. "I'll open 'er up for ye, if ye like."

The guard paused and looked closely at each man. Naron intensified the use of his gift on the guard. "Very well, then," the guard said at last. "Be on your way."

The three men boarded the sailing ship, Red Dragon, and then they carried their bags and the trunk down to their cabin.

"Cast off!" shouted the captain. "All hands to your stations!"

As am'Oranth, the first moon, rose like a glowing ghost above the horizon, the Red Dragon sailed southeast on en'Edlia Bay with its precious cargo. Naron, the self-made brains of the kidnapping, stood on deck. The cool, sea breeze blew his long, ebony hair back from his angular, narrow face. His eyes reflected the darkness. Naron pulled his calf-length, black coat closer around him and smiled wickedly. It was all going as he planned.

Phyre Jewl

CHAPTER 3

The twins called and searched for their brother. "He won't answer, even if he hears us," Jewl told her sister. Now, even with the glowing Scarlett Sinepa Scones scattered around the garden, it was too dark for them to keep peering into bushes to find their brother on their own. After more than an hour, Jewl and Phyre returned to the palace to alert their parents that Thairyn had run off.

"What happened?" boomed their broad-shouldered father, Merrick, the high patriarch of en'Edlia. He bellowed for the palace guard, his dark eyes flashing, and his still-young face lined with concern.

Phyre began to explain, but then she burst into tears. Her mother, Crown Matriarch Krystin, drew her daughter into her arms as the twins' grandmother, High Matriarch Narrian entered the main hall to see what was going on. Narrian's silver-streaked, dark hair was piled atop her head in an intricately braided design. She wore a grand gown of dark emerald on her erect, slender figure. She was always there to help with her grandchildren or the affairs of the realm as needed.

Jewl threw herself down in a chair in a huff. *Why does Thairyn always do this?* Jewl fumed to herself. *Why did I have to have a little brother? All I hear is 'I'm the crown patriarch,' and 'I have invisible magic.' He's just a bothersome brat. Why couldn't he have been a girl? Mother and Father always make us play with him. Well, I'm tired of it. He gets all the attention around here.*

The palace erupted in a frenzy of guards and servants. Jewl scowled at her grandmother, and then her mother, who were both fussing over her sister.

Feeling ignored by everyone, Jewl sighed crossly. She stood and headed for her chambers up the grand, central staircase. Jewl could hear the cries of Phyre and her mother's murmuring voice trying to comfort her sister. *What about me?* she thought angrily. The pounding of boots, as the palace guard hurried out to search for her brother, beat in time with her heart. The echoing of her father's voice through the palace felt like drumming in her head.

Jewl wasn't scared or hurt. She wasn't sad or worried. She was angry. She wished to shut out all the noise that Thairyn had caused. She stepped inside her chamber and threw the door shut with a resounding bang, which echoed back to the main hall. Many servants and soldiers paused, glanced up briefly, and then scurried on to their assigned duties. Jewl would have smiled to see she had finally gotten some attention, no matter how brief.

"I wish I had a better birth-gift!" Jewl raged. "I wish I could do something on my own. I am cursed with a birth-gift that relies on someone else's. I can't just fly away like Uncle Jarrius or call down swarms of bugs like Uncle Wayen. It's not fair! Even the gardener has a better birth-gift than me!"

Sitting down on her bed, Jewl remembered how Tesh, the gardener, had helped her use her birth-gift, along with his own, to create a new flower. They named it 'Jewl' for her. Tesh had placed his gentle, skilled hands on her shoulders, so she could access his power to manipulate plant life. She had been delighted with the deep purple color of the bloom she had begun to form in her hands. The stamens popped out in all directions, and she touched each one with bright, yellow thoughts. Her small fingers drew out four long, barely curving petals into a bell shape. Then, on a whim, she had pulled out one more, stretching it out and moving it downward. She widened and rounded its tip, cupping it into a ladle-like bowl. It was big enough to catch water to feed the smaller birds and insects. She liked the thought of that.

Then, Jewl gently touched the flower's deep throat and thought about the color of the sky. Jewl grinned as the deep purple throat lightened and softened to the turquoise-blue of a summer's afternoon. Jewl streaked this blue down the longer petal in three squiggly lines and into the bowl at the end. She gasped with delight at the sight of it.

Glancing up at Tesh, and noticing his short, mousy-brown hair was disheveled as always, Jewl looked for his approval. He nodded, smiling broadly.

"Truly a work of art! Are you finished?" he asked gently, his pale-blue eyes sparkling.

Turning back to her work, Jewl paused to appraise it herself. "Oh! It's missing a smell!" she replied. Jewl closed her eyes. She thought of warm, sweet smells, like just-baked muffybread and hot sweetwater with zulijuice. Then, she could actually smell those aromas wafting up from the blossom before her. "Mmmmmmmm!" She drew in the fragrance deeply.

Tesh chuckled. "Now are you finished?" he asked.

Jewl looked at her flower again. Suddenly, she had a wonderful idea. With one finger, she carefully touched the longer petal just above the bowl, and there she added a spot of pure crystalline, sparkling like a drop of rain in the sun. This was its jewel. Now it was finished!

"Amazing!" Tesh praised her. "I should have you work with me more often."

The experience had been like molding clay and painting with her mind. She had loved it. However, as soon as Tesh's hands moved off her shoulders, she was again powerless to do any magic. That was the nature of her birth-gift. She only had power through others. It wasn't fair. It wasn't right for someone in the ruling patriarchal family to have such a dependent birth-gift.

She lay back on her bed as her mother's voice came into her mind. "Jewl, you must be thankful you have a birth-gift, and you must be nice about it too. Too often, you remind your sister that you have magic, and she does not. That is hurtful and not becoming of a daughter of the high patriarch."

Now it seemed her brother, Thairyn, had no birth-gift either. Most children on Irth came into their gifts by the time they were three years old, or at the very latest, by the age of five. Thairyn was already seven. He was born in en'Edlia on Irth, unlike Jewl and her sister, who were born in Lyndell on their mother's magicless world. His time had passed for showing a birth-gift sign, though their parents still hung onto a hope that it would come. Father was very disappointed. He hadn't said so, but Jewl could tell he had hopes for a son with a powerful gift like his.

With no showing from Thairyn, the rebellious Xens had taken up a renewed cry against the non-magical members of the ruling family. They were demanding an heir to the crown, born of Irth, who possessed magic, and their threats were growing bolder.

Sometimes Jewl wished she had no birth-gift. It might be easier to deal with none than one so confining. Phyre was just too nice about their difference. She was kind and patient, gentle and compassionate. Tesh was teaching her about plants and healing. Jewl wished Phyre were more like her. If Phyre had a birth-gift, they could share it. That would be fun. No one would know which one was doing what.

There was one more thing that bothered Jewl. No one had spoken to her directly about it, but she had heard it talked of in quiet conversations not meant for her ears. The fact was, if neither Thairyn nor Phyre had birth-gifts, the official position of crown matriarch and eventual ruler of en'Edlia would fall on her shoulders at her grandmother's death. This frightened her more than anything else. According to the current laws of en'Edlia, the high patriarch or matriarch who ruled must have a birth-gift. Father had said it had always been that way, and that is what the Xens wanted now. *What about what I want?* thought Jewl. *Does anyone even care?*

"Why couldn't Thairyn have his silly, old, invisible magic, anyway? Then I could stop hearing about it!" she said aloud, and then she punched her pillow. *I would be glad,* she thought to herself, *not to be responsible for things that frighten me.* "How am I supposed to know how to rule?" Getting attention was one thing, but being in charge was quite another.

Thairyn seemed like he wanted to be high patriarch someday. Jewl was happy to let him. She just hated all his bragging about his imagined, invisible birth-gift.

Jewl slowly got out of her soiled dress and put on her bed-clothes. She unbraided her long, dark hair and began to brush it. The maids, Boolie and Leesel, would be fussing over her in a few moments, along with Murm bringing a snack and a warm drink to lull her off to sleep. Jewl loved all the maids, but she was not in the mood for company.

"Even the servants have more magical power than me," she cried, throwing her pillow with annoyance.

An irritating prickle in the back of her mind kept bothering her. She was worried about her brother. Jewl frowned. "He's such a breakfast bug!" she muttered. Then one corner of her mouth turned up. She really did love him, even if he was as bothersome as a swarm of slappers.

Jewl's mother and sister came quietly through the bedchamber door. Phyre's face was streaked with tear tracks. Her mother looked tired and worried. Jewl was suddenly aware of how much Phyre looked like their mother, even though Phyre had red hair, and her mother was blond like Thairyn.

"Did they find him yet, Mother?" Jewl asked. Her mother just shook her head as she helped Phyre get undressed for bed. Jewl wanted to talk more with her mother, but didn't know how to begin, so she waited and watched.

Jewl had always thought her mother was beautiful. Even now, with worry on her face, and trying to comfort a distraught daughter, she looked lovelier than the shimmering, sapphire gown she wore. Her long, blond braid slipped down over her shoulder as she leaned forward to caress Phyre's flushed cheeks. Though the twins' mother wore no crown most times, her fine manner proclaimed her royalty.

"Mother," Jewl tried again.

Just then, the maids came in with warm water, washing cloths, and sweet-smelling snacks. Jewl sighed. Usually she would place a hand on Boolie, teasingly using the maid's birth-gift to change the color or style of the maid's clothes, but tonight her heart wasn't in it. She ate quietly, accepted Leesel's washing without complaint, and crawled into her bed.

As the maids scuttled off to other business, Grandmother Narrian joined the twin's mother, and together they tucked the girls in. After giving each twin a kiss on the forehead, their mother and grandmother turned to leave the room.

"Mother?" Phyre called, sitting up. "Will you wake us when they find Thairyn?"

"No, you need your rest," she replied.

"Grandmother, will you live a long time?" Jewl suddenly asked.

Narrian smiled and chuckled. "What kind of question is that?"

"Sleep now, girls," their mother said. "All will be well in the morning. You'll see." Then she turned and pulled the door shut on her way out.

"But Grandmother . . ."

Narrian poked her head into the room again, her silvered hair catching the light. "I will live as long as I am supposed to. We'll talk more in the morning, Jewl. I love you both," she said, then closed the door.

The inner palace had quieted down for the night, but Jewl knew the search for her brother was still going on, and would continue until he was found, even if it took all night.

"Jewl," Phyre's soft voice interrupted her thoughts. "Do you think Thairyn will be all right?"

"Of course," Jewl responded, trying to sound cheerful.

"I can't help being scared for him," Phyre continued. "I have a strange feeling something bad has happened."

"Don't worry. The guards will find him." Jewl sounded confident, but she didn't feel it. "Commander Arreshi is good at her job. Mother said all would be well in the morning."

Phyre had exhausted herself with stressful fretting and crying. She lay back and was soon asleep. Jewl lay awake long after that. Phyre's words kept repeating in her head. *Something bad has happened.* She turned over again, staring into the dark. *Why haven't they found him yet?*

CHAPTER 4

Thairyn had been on a ship before, but he had always been able to look out at the horizon and have the fresh air on his face. Now he was cooped up in an old, musty trunk, inside a dusty, moldy sack, and trussed up like a wild meadow cock ready to be roasted. He was on the verge of being sick with the stench of his confinement space and the motion of the ship. He was too hot. His mouth was dry and tasted awful from the gag. There was not enough air. He sneezed again at the smell of dust and mold. His muscles were beginning to cramp, and his feet and hands were slowly going numb.

Will they ever come back for me? Thairyn worried. *Are they just waiting until the ship is in deep water to throw me overboard, trunk and all? Where are they going? What are their plans?* His head spun with questions he had no answers to and fears he couldn't seem to control.

Thairyn wiggled as much as he could to try to help the circulation in his hands and feet. Mostly it just made the pain of his bindings worse. In the confines of the trunk, he lay on his side, his legs doubled up to his chest, and his head bowed down. There was no way to be comfortable.

What about my family? he thought again. *Are they looking for me? How can they find me?* His panic surfaced again, and his heart contracted with fear. He began to scream and wriggle about in the trunk. Perhaps, if he made enough noise, someone would help him.

Thairyn suddenly heard muffled voices. He quieted to listen. The cabin door opened and closed, followed by the sound of heavy-booted feet. *Someone did hear!* he thought, full of sudden hope. He continued his tirade, hoping for rescue.

"Better get that brat out of there before he dies and is no good to us at all," Naron ordered in a low voice, giving the trunk a hearty kick. "Keep him tied up and quiet. We don't want nobody knowing."

With the force of Naron's blow, Thairyn's heart sank once again as he realized it was only the return of his captors. At least he was getting out of the trunk.

"How long to port?" That was Arth's voice.

"Tomorrow, late afternoon," answered Naron. "I've got a wagon and hordle all arranged for us there. We'll travel till after dark to get a good start."

"What about the boy then?" Tindus asked.

"We'll keep him in the trunk until we leave the city. After that, it will be up to the boy how he travels," Naron sneered.

"What about the ransom?" questioned Tindus, his eyes sparkling with greed.

"The ransom demands will be delivered tomorrow and the day after. Fhelda and Leebus will see to it."

Tindus gasped. "What? Ye let yer aunt—?"

"No, bumphead!" growled Naron. "She knows nothing."

"I like Fhelda," mumbled Arth.

"Ye would," Naron said, frowning.

"Down the coast then, is it?" Arth questioned.

16

"That it is, and quickly too. Get to it then. We have a long way to go before this is over."

Thairyn had heard every word. Now he knew they wanted him alive, which was a relief. *But where were they going?* He hadn't paid much attention in his geography class. *Down the coast somewhere. But which coast and how far?*

The rattling of the metal key in the lock of the trunk gave Thairyn a surge of hope. It clicked open, and cool air rushed in as the trunk lid was lifted.

"Hey, boy! Ye still alive?" Arth said, poking him hard through the sack. Thairyn grunted in response.

"Oh, good, ye are." Arth smiled and grabbed the sack that held the captive.

Thairyn felt himself lifted out of the trunk, and then he was dropped onto a much softer surface. The sack was untied, and Arth dumped him out onto the lower bunk in the cabin.

Thairyn wanted to cry and laugh at the same time. He was free of the confining trunk and dusty sack and their wretched smells, but it hurt to stretch out from his cramped position. He squinted in the brighter light. He groaned and winced, sneezed and coughed. At least breathing was easier, but his bindings still burned his wrists and ankles, and his legs were painfully tingling.

"Enjoy the comfort while ye can, brat," Naron whispered harshly. "Ye'll get the floor tonight, if yer lucky."

Thairyn glanced up at the third man now, seeing him for the first time. Naron was slender yet nearly as tall as Arth. He had black hair slicked back in a ragged mozer-tail and tied with a thin strip of leather. His calf-length, heavy coat and knee-boots were also black. His face was lean and cruel looking. His features were sharp and angular. Under a heavy brow, his brown eyes gave him a hawk-like look. His mouth was drawn down in a scowl. Thairyn knew this man was not going to be kind.

Thairyn arched his back and rolled over toward the wall of the cabin. He wanted to be away from the menacing countenance of this man, Naron.

"Watch him careful, lads. He's our ride to riches," Thairyn heard Naron say as the man left the cabin. The boy lay quietly listening as the two other men began to talk.

17

"Why do we have to watch the brat while he goes on deck?" complained Tindus. "I'm taking the bunk tonight, Arth. Ye can sleep on the floor with the boy."

"Whatever ye say, Tindus," said Arth slowly. "I'm used to it."

"I'm getting some sleep." Tindus yawned. "If I know Naron, he'll have me out all night on the road after we dock. Ye have first watch. If the brat causes any trouble, put him back in the trunk." Tindus shoved Thairyn painfully in the back with his boot. "Ye got that, brat?" Then he hoisted himself into the upper bunk.

"I hate sailing," Tindus mumbled, kicking off his boots, which heavily thudded on the floor.

"Ey, watch it!" Arth called out.

Thairyn jumped at the sudden noise. His heart was beating fast, and tears clouded his vision.

Arth took up his watch sitting on the floor with his back against the wall and his face towards the bunks.

The ship gently rocked and creaked, while sailors above board went about their duties. Tindus was soon snoring noisily with nothing showing out of his blanket except his gray, spiky hair.

Thairyn rolled over, wiping his face on the rough blanket beneath him as he did. He looked at Arth and tried to talk through the gag-rag but choked. "No talking now," warned Arth quietly. Thairyn held out his feet, gazing pleadingly at Arth.

"Ye'll be untied tomorrow, Naron says. If ye can be a good boy and not run away." Arth's large, round face crinkled up sympathetically as if he was looking at a newborn ruglump. "Do ye think ye can do that?" the big man asked gently.

Thairyn didn't know how to respond. Arth's words made him angry. He wanted to run away from these ruffians. He wanted to yell for help. He wanted to kick and scream until they took him back home, but he knew they weren't about to do that. No, they would keep him tied up for sure if he even attempted anything. He couldn't trust himself just yet to be 'a good boy,' so he shrugged in response.

"I'm sorry we have to be so mean. I like little ones," continued Arth. "I know! I'll tell ye a story. Would ye like that?"

Thairyn gave a weak nod as his mind began to whirl around an idea. It seemed this big man liked him in some way. He would have to think about how to make a friend out of Arth. He studied Arth's face. His hair was sandy-blond and hung straight and shaggy over his ears, down on his neck and forehead. His eyes were small and dark. His mouth was broad, filled with crooked teeth. His skin was tanned. Unshaven stubble covered his jaw and neck. Overall, it was a pleasant face and somewhat rugged looking. Thairyn noticed the creases in Arth's face. More lines made smiles than frowns. Aunt Nizza had taught him about creases. Creases can show character. Thairyn judged Arth to be of better character than Naron or Tindus.

Thairyn thought if he had someone on his side, it would mean better odds and a better chance of escape. It might take some time, but Thairyn began right then to work on his plan even if it was a very small one. His father had always said a plan hatching is better than no plan at all.

Seated on the wooden-planked floor of the tiny cabin, Arth straightened his brown and green, loose-woven jacket and crossed his legs beneath him. Once settled, the big man took a deep breath and launched into a tale of pirates, dragons, and adventures on the high seas. The villains were the heroes in these tales! It was nothing like Thairyn had ever heard at home, especially since Arth could change his face to match the characters of the stories. The boy began to enjoy the stories as his mind turned to imagining—heroic pirates harassed by the cruel authorities; evil dragons turned to treasure hording; ugly princes holding beautiful hostages. Arth's voice was deep and soothing and, what with the rocking of the ship, Thairyn soon drifted off to sleep.

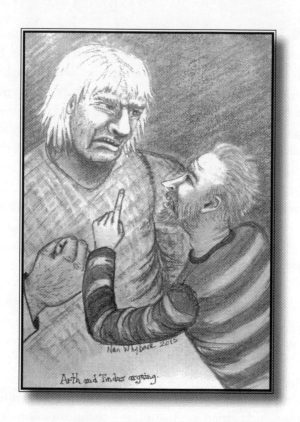

Arth and Tindus arguing.

CHAPTER 5

Thairyn woke to the men's harsh, arguing voices. Disoriented by the voices, and by waking up on a hard, wooden floor which was rocking, he kept his eyes closed, trying to let his head clear. He felt stiff. The painful bonds of rope on his wrists and ankles didn't allow him to move much. He wanted to cry, but he bit the gag instead, focusing on the terse voices overhead.

"I'll not let ye do it!" Arth's voice boomed.

"Silence! Ye'll follow orders, or feel the touch of me dagger 'tween yer ribs!" Naron threatened.

"But, Naron, he's just a wee lad!" Arth argued.

"And ye have a wee brain!" Tindus retorted. "I told ye he was soft on the brat!"

"I may like little ones, but I'm smarter than ye, Tindus! And I'll thank ye—"

"I wasn't the one making up bedtime stories, now was I, ye big bumphead!"

"Well, I wasn't the one snoring!"

Their arguing continued until Naron cursed them both and left the cabin.

That day dragged on as Thairyn drifted in and out of sleep. It was hard to do anything else bound up as he was. The soft-blue fossi-shell light never changed in the windowless cabin, so Thairyn had no idea how many hours had passed, or even if it was night or day. His captors never left him alone. However, Naron rarely came to the cabin, and Tindus escaped whenever he could. That left Arth, who seemed to be the boy's appointed guardian.

Arth told Thairyn stories to pass the time when the two of them were alone. During those times, Thairyn tried encouraging Arth to release him, with painful-sounding groans and tears. Once, as Arth gave in and moved forward to loosen the bonds, Tindus burst through the cabin door. He was swearing and angry, muttering on about how much he hated being bossed around by Naron. Arth quickly moved away, but still Tindus questioned him. Thairyn never got the big man to try again.

Now, the men's renewed argument roused the boy again. Though he knew not the day or time, he had learned it wise to pretend to sleep so he could listen to his captors' talk.

"Silence! Both of ye!" Naron hissed. "Or I'll cut out yer tongues and use 'em for fish bait. We don't want the boy knowing what's in store, or the whole crew either!"

Arth and Tindus ceased their arguing, only after muttering a few murderous words to each other. Naron continued in a deadly whisper.

"I'm the boss here! Ye'll carry out the plan like I made it, or so help me, I'll send ye to the depths of the sea to feed the bottom spiders. Now listen up! We'll be putting ashore at Bay's Port late in the day, and I've arranged transportation for us, like I said. We'll be well away from the port before Fhelda sends the first catlin with the ransom message. We'll—"

"What about—" Tindus interrupted.

"Silence, ye eel, and let me finish!" Naron seethed. There was a deadly pause. Then some scuffling around, and Naron continued in a whisper. "We'll be in Ner'ad by the next morning, and Dragon's Landing the day after. Then we'll get a boat to Claw Island," Naron explained.

"How long do we have to hole up there?" Tindus whined.

"Just until the ransom is paid. Then we kill the boy and—"

"Ye didn't say nothing about killing!" Arth burst in.

"Quiet!" Naron growled.

"Tindus never said killing was part of this." Thairyn heard Arth's sympathetic voice.

On the floor, with his back to the men, Thairyn's eyes had flown open at the mention of his imminent death. Fortunately, his gag prevented his gasp from being heard. *They are going to kill me!* he thought. *I have to get loose, get away. Oh, Father, I wish you were here now! Where are you?*

Naron's voice turned cold and venomous. "We're not keeping him, and we're not giving him back so he can become a big crown."

"I'm not keeping no brat!" Tindus spat out.

"But, Naron, I won't—" Arth began to object again.

There were more scuffling sounds, then Naron's hissing whisper. "The boy dies, and ye'll be doing it or I'll kill ye first, and then do it meself," Naron hissed. "I wants the high patriarch himself and his witch-woman to feel the sting and know I mean what I says. Now shut yer yap." Heavy feet stumbled back. Thairyn felt the jarring motion through the floorboards. Thairyn began to worry someone would step on him in the men's tussling.

"Brains of a breakfast bug!" Tindus muttered, while Arth remained silent.

Naron's voice continued then. "We'll be off on the first ship to the City of the Lost. We'll lay low there. Then I'm going back to en'Edlia to make sure there are no heirs from that witch-woman to take the throne, magic or not. The Xens will keep me informed, but I don't trust any of them to do the job right.

"Now wake up the little crown. We're coming into port soon. Get him into the trunk and make sure he keeps quiet. I'm going topside." Naron left the cabin, banging the door loudly.

Thairyn slowly turned over, making a show of waking up so Tindus didn't kick him again. Arth frowned at the boy sadly. Tindus scowled and ran his slender, gnarled fingers through his short, graying hair. "Well, ye heard the boss! Get him ready to move."

Arth knelt down, picked Thairyn up, and carefully laid him on the bunk. He checked over the ropes binding the captive and the gag to see if it was still in place. While Tindus was busy pulling on his boots and striped shirt, Arth leaned low over Thairyn's ear and whispered, "I'll not hurt ye, boy, just trust me. I'll be gentle with ye."

"Stop that!" Tindus yelled and shook his head. He pulled on his long, sharp nose.

"I wasn't doing nothing," shot back Arth. "Little ones need gentle care."

"May as well give him gentleness now for all the good it will do him later," Tindus sneered, showing his missing front tooth as he scratched at his short, pointed beard.

"I said don't talk about it!" warned Arth, changing his face to look like Naron for a moment.

"Sea slugs!" Tindus rolled his eyes. "Get the brat in the trunk so we can be off this stinking barrel." He stomped out of the cabin and slammed the door.

Alone with Thairyn, Arth shook his head and looked down at the boy. "I'm sorry, little crown. I don't know how I got into this. Thought it might be fun, get some pa'trees to fill me empty purse. Tindus is me friend. He's helped me many times. I thought it was me time to help him, but I didn't know what Naron planned. Friend or no friend, I've no taste for this."

Arth picked Thairyn up and placed him in the trunk. Thairyn mumbled through the gag trying to keep Arth's attention, but Arth just shook his head. "I swear I'll get ye out as soon as I can," he said. The light disappeared as Arth shut the trunk. The key clicked in the lock.

Thairyn dreaded the dark confinement of the trunk, but could do nothing to stop it. At least he was free of the dust-laden sack. So far, Arth's fear of Naron was greater than his caring for him. Thairyn thought about how he had run away from his sisters. It was almost funny that he was hiding and caught at the same time. He thought about Arth. Thairyn would have plenty of time to think about what to do next, if he ever got out of the trunk again.

Thairyn's stomach lurched as he felt Arth hoist the trunk onto his shoulder, then move out of the cabin, jolt up some stairs, sway across the ship's deck, and later, wobble down the gangplank onto the shore of Bay's Port.

* * *

The Red Dragon had come along the pier at Bay's Port two hours before twilight the second day. Naron had had plenty of time before dark to find his contact with the hordle and wagon, obtain a few provisions, and be a few miles down the coast. The coast road south was narrow and winding; at times there were steep drop-offs where the land had tumbled into the sea. More than a few had taken a misstep in the fog or dead of night. Their bones, picked clean by tidewaters and scavengers, littered the rocks along with shells and driftwood.

Naron guided the dirty-tan colored hordle and rumbling, three-sided wagon down the road, while Tindus briskly strode in front, keeping them on the path. Tindus's birth-gift was his night-vision. He could see like a catlin at night. Arth rode in the wagon with the supplies, holding the trunk securely to lessen the jostling the boy inside would have to endure.

Naron did not want to attract attention with torches or fires. He had picked his accomplices well. He had planned each detail skillfully. They would be in Ner'ad by first light, then on to Dragon's Landing. If they made good time, he might make camp between the two, if there was a secluded area well off the road. He had no doubt Tindus could find one for them.

Naron grinned to himself. The ransom was nearly his.

CHAPTER 6

Tindus marched on several dozen paces ahead of the wagon He
was enjoying his bit of solitude. The night was very dark, but
Tindus's night vision allowed him to see as clearly as if it were
day. He thought back to his youth, when he had slipped away from
his meager house alone many times to enjoy the quiet of the night
away from his bickering family. He gazed up at the stars and took a
deep breath. He found comfort in the constant stars and the dark that
enfolded him like a blanket. He strode on confidently, lost in thought.

Suddenly he realized he wasn't hearing the wagon's creak and rattle anymore. Gazing over his shoulder, he shook his head, scratched his beard, and walked back to the stationary wagon.

Naron had nodded off. The reins were slack in his hands, and the hordle had slowed and eventually stopped on the dark, quiet sea road to Ner'ad. Several hours had passed since the sun went down. The moon, am'Oranth, was in crescent phase, shining dimly.

Now, grasping the hordle's bridle, Tindus led the weary beast and dusty wagon off the road, through a tall-grass meadow, and behind a small stand of ragged-looking sea pines. Tindus looked up at Naron's shadowed face. "Bumphead!" he said, frowning. Then, he took great pleasure in pulling the dozing Naron off the wagon seat onto the ground.

*   *   *

Thairyn jerked awake to Naron's cursing tirade and Tindus' laughter. Anyone within a mile of them would have heard the ruckus, except for the constant crashing waves and the steady, whooshing of the breeze through the pines that carried their voices off like ghosts in a whirlwind.

Once it had turned dark, and it was evident there would be few by-passers, Arth had opened the trunk. He had asked Naron if he could untie the boy, but Naron refused. "Don't want to lose our money in the dark, now do we?" was his response.

After everyone's rude awakening, Naron ordered Tindus to make a quick, rough campsite and Arth to stay in the wagon with the boy. Naron assigned Tindus as guard for the night. "Ye can sleep all day for all I care," Naron told him. "But if I find ye sleeping when I wake up, I'll kill ye."

Now, Thairyn lay on his side in the open trunk in the back of the wagon, with Arth snoring beside him. The big man had his arm wrapped protectively around the base of the trunk to keep it steady.

Thairyn had never slept outside before. It was so dark! He couldn't see anything beyond his own nose. He lay listening to the ocean's thunder, the meadow bugs' chirping, and the whooshing of the wind through the grasses and trees. He could smell the salt in the air, the bruised, windswept pines, and the restless dust from the road. It felt calm, yet wild; quiet, yet full of sounds; friendly, yet scary.

It was one of those rare nights, when only the first moon was out and the second moon, ul'Damen, was in its new phase and invisible to the eye. Thairyn wriggled himself over so he could gaze at the heavens. The sky was black velvet strewn with gleaming crystals. It made Thairyn feel very small and alone. Again, he thought of his family. What were they doing? Were they still looking for him? *I guess I am the champion of catch-me-if-you-can*, he thought sadly. *I am hidden so well, no one will ever find me.*

A tear trickled down his face and into his ear. It made him mad that he couldn't wipe it out, so he kicked at the trunk with all his might. *I hope I break it to bits! I want to get out of here!* Then, realizing he might attract some unwanted attention, he lay still again.

His belly gurgled and grumbled. His mouth was so dry. On the ship, Arth had slipped him a mouthful or two of water and two bites of mozer cheese by pulling the tied cloth up and pushing the gag to one side. It was better than nothing, but a poor substitute for a nice, long drink of cool water and a full meal. Thairyn had never been so hungry or thirsty in his life.

The young crown patriarch was suddenly flooded with emotions. He was frightened of his captors, yet angry with them too. He was feeling stupid and helpless, and terrified of never seeing his family again. Worst of all, a great hopelessness was welling up inside him; a despair so tangible he could feel it coming like a big, black thing with gaping jaws slowing rising beneath him. A shiver ran through him. The thing would soon swallow him whole. If that happened, he knew he would probably just die.

Overhead, a flock of Irth Stars swirled through the night sky. The birds' soft-orange glow was warm and somehow comforting as they swarmed and swooped in the night. Thairyn watched them soaring freely and easily through the open skies. He envied their freedom.

Right then, Thairyn made a decision. *Am I crown patriarch or not? What would Father do? What would he say to me right now?* He'd say, *"Thairyn, it's all up to you. You can't worry about what you don't have. Just do what you can with what you have, and make it your best."* He decided he was not going to lie there any longer and let that dark monster of despair take him. He didn't want to die. If he could get free from his bonds, he could steal away and hide. He was good at hiding. Maybe he could talk Arth into coming with him. If that didn't' work, he might have to go along with his captors. Wherever they wanted to go, whatever they wanted to do, he would do too. He would become a thief like Arth. Perhaps then they would let him live. It had to be better than being tied up and stuffed in a trunk for the rest of his life. Though, there might not be much of that left either.

Thairyn also decided to try to free himself, just in case he could. This was the first time no one was watching him closely, and the trunk lid was open. He set his feet against the inside of the trunk and pushed himself up, scooting and pulling himself into a sitting position. Then, he began rubbing his wrist bindings on the metal edging of the trunk latch.

Resting briefly from time to time, Thairyn worked steadily at it all night. The wagon sides were high enough that even sitting up, Thairyn's head didn't show above them. Tindus might have heard him if he had been close by, but he had gone off a ways in a huff. Besides, Thairyn knew Tindus cared little for what he did and paid no mind to his noises. Arth's snoring hid the swooshing sounds of the ropes very nicely.

As the eastern sky turned pink and then gold with the rising sun, Thairyn felt the slightest give in the ropes, and his heart leaped. Arth still slept, and the other men were out of sight. Thairyn felt damp with his exertion and the morning dew. His arms burned with exhaustion, but he kept up his movement as hope spurred him on.

Suddenly, Thairyn had a strange feeling. He looked around him. Dark eyes glared at him through the slats of the wagon-side. Looking into those eyes, he froze with fear.

"Getting resourceful, are we?" Naron's voice was quiet, yet cruel.

Thairyn had been so busy at his task, he hadn't noticed Naron's approach. Now he was caught. In a moment, Naron leaped into the back of the wagon, grabbed Thairyn's hands, and pulled them painfully up over the boy's head. Thairyn hollered through the gag. Then, he watched the man slowly pull his knife out from under his coat.

Now I'm going to die! thought Thairyn. *Oh, Arth! Wake up and save me!* He squeezed his eyes shut and held his breath, waiting for the fatal blow to strike him.

Just then, Arth moaned and rolled over, crashing into Naron, knocking him off his feet. Naron hit the wagon bed hard, and the sudden noise sent a flock of muffy birds to flight. That brought Tindus running and startling Arth into full wakefulness.

"What's the matter?" Tindus yelled out breathlessly.

"What's going on?" asked Arth, scratching his head and squinting in the brightening morning light.

Looking at Arth with terror in his eyes, Thairyn nodded toward Naron and tried to make a noise through the gag. Arth's gaze turned on Naron, and he saw the knife still in Naron's grip.

"Hey! What goes on?" the big man questioned Naron menacingly.

"I was just going to cut his ropes before ye interfered, ye big oaf!"

"It's about time," breathed Arth. He quickly grabbed the knife from Naron, cut the bindings from Thairyn's hands and feet, and then pulled the gag-rag from his mouth. "Sorry, little one," Arth lamented, seeing the red, raw skin the ropes had created. His face scrunched up in sympathy.

Thairyn was so relieved that he cried. He opened his mouth to thank Arth, but no sounds came out of his dry throat as the tears gushed from his eyes. His wrists and ankles stung and burned now that the air reached his rubbed-raw skin. His limbs were stiff and his shoulders ached. He was suddenly very weak from lack of food and his efforts through the night; he could do nothing but sit there, letting the tears slide down his checks. He knew now, even if he had broken his bonds, he would not have had the strength to run away.

"There's no trouble then? Just the brat as usual." Tindus mumbled. "And yer friend. Where'd ye—"

"I don't want to talk about it," Tindus huffed.

Suddenly, Arth was lifting Thairyn out of the trunk and carrying him from the wagon to a small stream nearby. The cool water stung the boy's skin, but he let the big man gently bathe his wounds and then lift water to his lips. Thairyn drank heartily. Water never tasted so good.

"Not too much at once or ye'll be sick," Arth warned, and pulled the boy away before his thirst was quenched.

"Hurry up! Stop babying him. We have to get," Naron snapped. "I want to be in Ner'ad afore nightfall."

Tindus broke camp after he and Naron had eaten a hasty meal of mozer jerky and sweet cloud fruit from the small bundle of supplies they had picked up at Bay's Port.

Arth gently carried Thairyn back to the wagon, and laid him in the bed. He rolled his coat and put it under Thairyn's head.

"Give him yer share of food," Naron growled at Arth. "He can ride there today, but tomorrow he will ride up here with me." Naron turned away, snapping the reins on the hordle's back. Tindus jumped into the bed too, and lay down to sleep the day away.

As the wagon rattled down the rocky, dirt road, the sun's rays slanted through the sea pines and the rising dust. Naron turned back to Arth. "Ye had better keep a close eye on the little crown. If he gets loose, the last thing ye'll be feeling is the stick of me knife."

Fheldah

CHAPTER 7

Fhelda stroked the flying catlin between its ears. Its black and white striped coat was silky smooth. She was lonely in her tiny shack in The Shards of en'Edlia. She had enjoyed the company of the catlin these last two days, so she was not wanting to send it away on her nephew's errand. Whatever it was.

Naron. Fhelda thought back through the past years. Her nephew was troubling. Naron had been very close to his grandfather, Zarcon, but his parents had wisely disassociated themselves with Zarcon when he had begun delving into the dark magics. She had taken Naron in after his parent's accidental death. Naron's anger and unhappiness had only increased when he learned of the death of his estranged grandfather shortly after that.

Fhelda shook her head at the memory of it all. Now she was Naron's only living relative. She was growing old and weary. She had done her best to console and counsel him, encouraging him to seek higher ways. In spite of all her efforts, he began to shun the light, seeking a darker path like his grandfather—sliding out at dusk like a shadow and reappearing at dawn. The angry boy became an angry young man.

One night Naron didn't come back. Then suddenly, he showed up at her door just after dark. Fhelda frowned as she recalled her conversation with Naron.

"Naron! Where have ye been? It's been months! I've been so worried."

"Never ye mind!" Naron dismissed her concern. "Bring me the old trunk. I have something I need ye to do."

"What? What is it? Are ye in trouble?"

Naron laughed bitterly at her. "I'm not a child anymore! I have me own business to tend to. Just get the trunk."

"But Naron, I—"

"Get the trunk, Auntie!"

When Fhelda returned dragging the old trunk to the door, Naron thrust a flying catlin into her arms.

"I want ye to keep this catlin for two days. On the morning of the third day, release it to deliver the message."

"That's all? That's what ye want me to do?"

"Do ye understand, Fhelda?"

"Yes, but . . ."

Naron quickly hefted the trunk onto his back, turned, and stalked off into the night's darkness.

"But what's in the message? Who's it for? Naron? Where are you going? Answer me! Naron! Come back!"

Fhelda had not seen her nephew since. Now it was the morning of the third day, and she was to release the catlin to deliver its message. In a ragged dress, she sat in her small, ramshackle house, the windows long since boarded over. She stroked the black-and-white patterned catlin on her lap. She wasn't in a hurry to do her nephew's bidding. She was disturbed by Naron's sudden appearance and then disappearance. Fhelda ran her fingers over the catlin thoughtfully. "And what trouble has Naron gotten into now?" she asked the winged creature. The catlin looked up at her and yowled softly.

Maybe she should take a peek at the message. It was concealed in the metal tube that lay neatly between the catlin's wings, held in place by a leather harness. She reached for the latch on the tube, but suddenly the catlin hissed and leapt away.

Fhelda tried catching the catlin for several minutes, all the while it hissed and ran from her. Careful to avoid the exposed seat springs, she finally flopped into her faded, old chair, wheezing for breath. Fhelda sighed as she watched the dust particles, stirred up by her scuttling about, settle back on everything. She silently cursed her nephew's mysterious errand.

When Fhelda had rested enough, she got up slowly and opened the door. The catlin sauntered toward it, flipping the end of its long tail wildly. The creature stopped in the doorway and looked up at Fhelda. "Well, go on with ye then," she sighed wearily.

Surprising to Fhelda, the catlin rubbed against her leg before leaping into the air and flying away. Fhelda just shook her head and closed the door.

Flying catlin

CHAPTER 8

The catlin flew a straight and speedy course. It had been somewhat irritated at the two-day delay after being hired. The unusual procedure had made it nervous. The woman had been calming though. The catlin had come to enjoy the bit of leisure, except at the last. What could that woman have been thinking trying to open the message compartment? Well, the catlin had taught her the proper way of it for sure. Rule Number 2: Once within the tube, no one sees the message except the person for whom it is meant. The woman would not soon forget that rule of messaging by flying catlin.

The catlin skimmed over rounded rooves and leafy treetops. It ignored the chattering birds that scolded when it came too close to their nesting sites. After gliding on the moist seaside air for several minutes, the catlin's destination came into view. The palace was immense. The high pale-gray stone walls and towering turrets shone in the sunlight. Here and there large, carved seashells adorned the structure and glistened with real iridescent, inlaid shells. The east side of the structure wandered down to the seaside and was battered by the crashing waves. Behind the palace, to the northwest, Tesh, the palace gardener, kept the fountains blubbing, meandering hedges trimmed, and acres of flowers always blooming. The front of the palace faced south toward en'Edlia Bay and the city. It had a broad, curving drive circling an expansive lawn area. Wide rows of steps led to the open, covered veranda, lined with columns. The nation's emerald flags fluttered in the off-shore breeze.

The catlin always enjoyed looking down on the palace, but now, released to its duty, nothing would distract it from completing its task—except perhaps a bit of fun. It was late morning, and the palace guards were still fresh and watchful on the steps of the veranda. All the more challenging for the catlin as it gained some altitude preparing to dive-bomb the hapless guards.

With a hair-prickling yowl, the catlin's path was like a frozen rope hurtling toward the sentries. One shouted a warning to ready the others for an attack. Just at the last second, the catlin flipped its tail and changed the angle of its wings. It whooshed overhead, narrowly missing the guards' ducking heads. As an added insult, the catlin kicked the hats off two guards with its hind feet, then rose in a vertical ascent toward the palace towers far above.

The catlin landed lightly on the windowsill of the patriarchal suite several stories up. Its throat rumbled in a contented purr as the guards' yells and curses rose to its ears. The catlin preened its iridescent black wings for a full minute, enjoying the scene below.

*   *   *

Jewl and her sister, Phyre, had been playing inside that morning, feeling the need to be close to their mother. Of course, their mother had told them she would not even consider letting them go outside to play. It had been two days, yet Thairyn had not been found.

Jewl sat in the family quarters with her book propped up, but not really seeing the words. She couldn't focus on anything. A gloom had settled over the palace, and it was depressing. She wanted everything to be back to normal. Why couldn't her brother just march through the door right now? There would be more crying and scolding for a while, but soon things would settle down, and her family could be happy again. *How long will this go on?* she thought. *Mother will die of grief. Phyre will die of guilt—of course she blames herself—and Father will have the whole of en'Edlia in the dungeons. What will become of me?* Jewl's thoughts wandered on and on.

The guards had searched for Thairyn the whole first night and into the next day. Merrick summoned the high council to a special session. They made plans to widen the search and take more precautions in guarding the palace occupants. The guard brought in people for questioning, and imprisoned some on suspicion. All of en'Edlia was being turned upside-down and shaken.

Then, the catlin arrived.

"I don't care who the high patriarch is in session with, I need him right now!" Jewl could hear the desperation in her mother's voice as she spoke to a servant. "This is urgent! Tell him there is a message about . . . our son!" Krystin's voice caught in her throat. The servant bowed and ran to fetch Merrick.

Phyre was trying to comfort their mother, who sat in a crumpled heap on the satin sofa with the message in her quivering hand. Jewl could see her mother hadn't been sleeping well. Krystin's usually immaculate dress was mussed, and her long, blond hair was disheveled. Jewl wished her Aunt Nizza was here. Her birth-gift brought warmth and happiness to others. They could really use it now. However, Nizza and Wayan had gone off-world to visit their other brother for several days.

The flying catlin sat calmly at their feet waiting for compensation. Grandmother Narrian entered the family's spacious chambers. "What now?" she asked, wringing her hands.

Krystin handed her the catlin's message. Narrian sat on the other side of Krystin and after reading the message, wrapped her arm around her daughter-in-law. "When will it end?" Narrian sighed. They all waited for Merrick in bitter silence.

It took quite a while, but finally, the twins' father, with Ardloh the Oracle in tow, burst into the family chambers.

"Oh, Merrick!" both the women cried at once.

"What is it? What's happened?"

"This came by catlin," Krystin replied weakly, handing the message to her husband. "They have him, Merrick. He's alive."

"Alive, but held captive, by the look of it," Merrick stated angrily. "How dare they! I'm sorry you had to read this, my darling," he huffed, and took his wife's hand.

Ardloh took the message then and read it aloud, while the couple held each other for comfort. *To the high patriarch and his witch: We have yer son. He is safe for now, but unless ye deliver a ransom of 75,000 pa'trees and meet our demands, ye will never see yer son again. Delivery must be by the next double moon's rise. Details and conditions will follow. Signed, The Thieves.*"

"Obviously they are of the Xen persuasion— not approving of a non-magical heir to the throne," Ardloh noted. "Who knows when you will hear more? Best pay off this catlin and send it away in case the next message is waiting for its return."

Jewl slid off her chair while the adults went into a quiet but intense discussion. She knelt by the catlin, stroking its smooth wings. "Do we have to send it away so soon?" she asked. Phyre looked over and frowned at Jewl's seeming lack of concern.

"Oh, Merrick! I can't imagine how scared Thairyn must be in the hands of those kidnappers, those evil men!" Krystin cried, her pretty face lined with worry. "What can we do? Can't we just give them what they want and get our boy back?"

"I think we must proceed with caution," Merrick said slowly. "We don't even know what all their demands are yet. Besides, giving in to their demands might open up a whole new market for the kidnapping of ruling family members. We must find them, if possible, before harm comes to Thairyn."

"But, Father!" Phyre gasped.

"Let me think," he muttered, running his hand through his short, dark hair, while pacing the room.

"What about the catlin?" Jewl mentioned again.

"The catlin?" Merrick stopped and looked down at his daughter. "The catlin! Yes! Jewl, I love you!"

"I love you, too," replied Jewl, looking confused. She twined her dark braid around her fingers.

"What are you talking about?" Krystin asked.

"I can see into the catlin's mind and find out who sent it!" Merrick explained.

"Brilliant!" Ardloh stated.

The high patriarch moved to pick up the catlin, but it hissed and moved away. "Blast these wretched beasts!" he cried. "As much as we use them around here, they still don't like me for some reason."

"I can help," said Jewl. She gently plucked up the catlin and sat with it on her lap.

"Of course you can!" Her father smiled at her.

Jewl loved when her father smiled at her. It made everything right in the world. She wanted to help everyone be happy. Maybe this would be the way.

Merrick stood behind Jewl and placed his hands gently on her shoulders so she could use his birth-gift. As she felt the flow of power, she looked deeply in the large, yellow eyes of the catlin and probed into its memory. "I see a dark, hooded face. I can't make it out," she began, still stroking the catlin.

"Now I see a small run-down house. It must be The Shards."

Ardloh chuckled. "What place in The Shards isn't run-down?"

"Quiet!" shushed Krystin.

"There's an old woman with a sad, wrinkly face. I see her petting the catlin. Now she is chasing it! How strange. Now she is letting it leave the house."

There was silence in the room for several moments. Jewl continued to gaze into the catlin's mind.

"I can see the path the catlin flew to reach the palace. Now it's diving at the guards!" Jewl giggled, and her father lifted his hands from her. The sudden removal of her father's large, warm hands and the loss of his great magic left Jewl feeling light and empty for a moment. She shivered.

"We must bring this woman in for questioning," her father proclaimed. "Jewl, look at me." Jewl turned to face her father and gazed into his deep, brown eyes. She felt him enter her mind to see the information she had just gained from the catlin. He seemed to study everything intently for a moment, and then he withdrew. He marched to the door and quickly pulled it open.

"Summon Commander Arreshi and Rewl at once!" the high patriarch commanded the servant outside the door. "Have them meet me in the diplomat's conference room immediately." Merrick then drew a map of the catlin's route to the palace to give to Commander Arreshi.

"What will you do?" Krystin asked.

Merrick looked up from his drawing. "With this map, we can find where the woman lives who sent the catlin. I called for Rewl, the artist, so I can project into his mind the image of this woman, and he can draw it. If we cannot locate her at the house, we will post her picture everywhere, so all will be on the lookout for her. She won't get away."

"I just hope she knows where Thairyn is," Phyre said softly.

"Me, too," said Krystin.

"Thank you, Jewl," her father said, hugging her. "You may have helped your brother very much." He then hurried away with the oracle trailing behind.

Jewl felt warm and very grown up. Perhaps her birth-gift was useful after all. She turned toward her mother, smiling, just as her sister burst into tears again. The startled catlin jumped to the floor.

"Oh, Mother! Not The Shards!" Phyre cried. "Not that terrible, awful place! Poor Thairyn!" She buried her face in her mother's lap, while Krystin stroked her ginger-colored hair.

Jewl's smile turned to a frown. *More crying. Just when I was beginning to feel better,* she thought bitterly. She slumped down in the chair, and the catlin jumped back into her lap.

"Oh, the catlin!" exclaimed her grandmother. "Shall I take care of it?"

Krystin looked up. "Thank you, Narrian. In the drawer, over there," she pointed toward a huge, richly carved chest of drawers with golden shell handles.

Narrian scooped a few coins from the drawer and placed them in the message tube, closing it securely. Immediately, the catlin jumped down and trotted to the window. Jewl was sorry to see it go. She liked the thought of having a pet. It seemed comforting in a way. She watched the catlin push behind the tapestry and heard it leap to the window ledge. There was a flutter of wings, and it was gone.

Jewl looked back at Phyre, whose green eyes were rimmed with red. When Jewl thought about it, she guessed Phyre was terrified at the thought of her brother being in The Shards. She remembered once,

Arreshi, commander of the palace guard, had told them what it was like in The Shards.

"The Shards," the commander stated, "is a place to be avoided. It is an unhealing wound in en'Edlia, dark and festering. It is filled with unsavory characters, like thieves and cutthroats as well as the poverty-stricken, disease-ridden, and drunkards. The Shards sleeps off its addictions during the day, but comes alive at night. It is a place for things thrown away or left behind, things nobody wants, things nobody cares about." Jewl shivered at the thought of such a horrible place. Now Arreshi would be going there to look for her brother.

Ardloh

CHAPTER 9

The high patriarchal family sat in their family quarters, convened at Ardloh the Oracle's request. It was late evening, and the palace had somewhat quieted for the night. Phyre sat anxiously waiting. She was keenly aware this meeting was not a usual occurrence. Thairyn had been missing for three nights now, and she feared bad news was coming.

The twins watched their father pacing while they waited for the oracle to come. Narrian and Krystin sat together, talking quietly. Jewl was looking wide-eyed, but Phyre was notably nervous.

"Merrick, please sit down," Narrian said. "I'm sure he will be here soon."

"I hope so," Krystin said. "The girls need to be in bed. Are you sure they need to be here?"

Merrick sat on the edge of a chair. "Ardloh said the whole family should come. He said it was very important."

"What about Uncle Wayen and Aunt Nizza?" asked Phyre.

"Ardloh said he could not wait for them to return from their visit to your other uncle," her father stated flatly.

"What do you think Ardloh wants to talk to us about, Father?" asked Jewl.

"I'm not sure. I hope he has some news about your brother."

The family sat for several more minutes, talking quietly. Phyre yawned as she thought about the last few days. Ever since the night Thairyn had disappeared, the palace had lost its calm sense of security. Servants were looking over their shoulders. Sentries were posted everywhere. Phyre didn't like being unable to play in the gardens, and her sister had been very vocal about their lack of freedom. It was hard to focus on her studies when the guards trooped strange people in and out of the interrogation room daily. The palace and city alike were as busy as a swarm of zippers.

Phyre laid her head in her mother's lap, enjoying this time of family closeness. She didn't understand why those thieves wanted her brother. Was it just to hurt her family? Why would they want to do that? She just couldn't understand that kind of hate.

Because of the kidnapping, her father had no time for her or Jewl. Her grandmother had stayed closer these days, which was a comfort. However, Phyre found her mother often distracted and anxious. She knew her mother was frightened, but weren't they all? Phyre wished for the millionth time that Thairyn would just walk through the door with Commander Arreshi, and life would return to normal.

Suddenly, there was a rap on the door. The talking stopped abruptly, their attention turning toward the sound. "Come!" Merrick called loudly.

The double doors opened wide, and a servant stepped in and bowed. "The Great Oracle, Ard—"

"Yes, yes!" Ardloh skirted the servant. "That's enough! Thank you." The oracle strode briskly into the room, his long, green robe swirling around him. Frowning, the servant backed out of the room and closed the doors.

Phyre had rarely spent time with the oracle and had mostly seen him in passing in the palace halls. Now she studied him closely.

Ardloh, the Great Oracle, was tall and slim, but broad shouldered. His short white hair and long beard shone around his face. His cheeks, now pink-tinged at the servant's remark, were high, almost bony. Under his downcast, cloud-like eyebrows, his eyes were pale blue and glistened with power and purpose. His emerald robe was embroidered at the hem and sleeves with gold symbols and runes from an ancient time. The staff in his hand was as tall as the oracle himself and finely carved with the emblem of en'Edlia's flying seashell at the top.

Phyre noticed that a certain warm, smoky, spicy smell always accompanied Ardloh and his apprentice when either of them came to visit. She wasn't sure what it was, but it was pleasant, and she liked it.

"Ardloh!" Merrick cried, moving to meet the oracle, who set his staff against the wall.

"Finally," Krystin sighed, looking tired herself.

Phyre sat up and tried to look more attentive, expectantly waiting for the oracle to begin. Her father didn't wait.

"What do you think, Ardloh?" Merrick questioned the oracle as they moved to join the family in the seating area of the spacious, lavishly-decorated room. "Have you had any revelation on Thairyn's whereabouts?"

"I have had a dream pointing me in a distinct direction," Ardloh stated.

Krystin sat forward eagerly. "What direction? Do you know where he is?"

The oracle's face grew solemn. He clasped his hands behind his back and turned away, walking toward the heavily draped windows. Being several floors up, the room had a grand view of en'Edlia Bay and the city. Drawing the plush draperies aside and looking out over the sea, Ardloh spoke without turning to face them.

"Do you know how much I love en'Edlia? I grew up here. Played in the bay and on the market streets when I was a boy. Was apprentice to the magnificent oracle, Wilcom. He was a truly great man. How I wish he could see me now." Ardloh chuckled sadly and turned around. "And now, I have been in the service of high patriarchal families for over two hundred years."

"Amazing!" cried Krystin.

"How old are you?" asked Jewl.

"That's not a polite question, dear," whispered her grandmother.

The oracle looked at Jewl, smiled slightly, and then replied, "My birth-gift and endowed powers as oracle have extended my life well beyond the average beings of this world. All oracles of Irth have had long lives of service to the realm."

"But what about Thairyn?" Phyre asked, more anxious to hear about her brother than the old man's past.

Ardloh gazed out the window a few more moments, and then moved toward the twins' father. He looked upon Merrick with love and admiration. Phyre saw tears well up in Ardloh's eyes. "How can I tell you such news?" he asked sadly.

"What . . . what is it?" Merrick gasped. "Is it Thairyn? Is he . . .?"

Krystin clung to Narrian, and Phyre clutched at her sister, all fearing the worst.

The oracle grasped Merrick by the shoulders. "Calm yourself." He looked over at the rest of them then, finally focusing on Krystin. "Your son is safe for now."

Everyone sighed. Krystin's tears started with relief. Merrick looked back to Ardloh and asked, "Then what is troubling you so, Ardloh, my dear friend?"

"Do you know where my brother is?" Phyre ventured.

"Is he in danger?" Jewl added.

Ardloh shook his head. "I do not know exactly where Thairyn is, but I do have two very important things to tell you."

The oracle released Merrick and clasped his hands behind his back again. "First, I feel you should send out the dragon riders, Merrick. They will aid you in your search now."

"Very well," replied the high patriarch. "I shall call them to service first thing tomorrow."

"The dragon riders!" whispered Jewl excitedly to Phyre.

"Second . . ." Ardloh looked at the floor a moment, and then continued. "I'm leaving en'Edlia for the Great Altere Mountains."

Merrick frowned. "Now is not a good time for a trip," he stated.

"We need you here," Krystin said, wiping her eyes. "Especially now with Thairyn missing."

"When will you return?" Merrick asked with concern.

"I'm not coming back," the oracle said quietly. Everyone's eyes focused on the oracle's face. There were gasps of surprise around the room.

Suddenly, Merrick laughed. "Of course you're coming back, you . . ." He stopped as he saw the truth in the oracle's face. Phyre saw a look come over her father she had never seen before. She wasn't sure exactly what it was. It looked a little like fear, but also wonder and disbelief. For just a moment, Phyre saw Thairyn's face in her father's expression.

"Is there something wrong?" Narrian stood up.

"Has someone mistreated you?" Krystin asked.

"Why are you leaving us, Ardloh?" Jewl questioned.

Again, the oracle smiled sadly, shaking his head. "Please, sit down." He motioned to all. "There is nothing wrong, except . . . I am dying."

Krystin and Narrian jumped up again in shock. Merrick gasped, "You are ill? Let me call the healers and—"

"No," the oracle stated firmly. "Not this time." He laid a hand on Merrick's shoulder. "The time has come for me to take my final journey. It will be one from which I will never return."

The high patriarch sat down heavily in a chair and looked up at Ardloh. "Are you certain?"

"My vision was clear. There is no mistake."

"But with Thairyn's kidnapping, we . . . I need you now more than ever," pleaded Merrick.

Phyre felt sorrier for her father right then than for anyone else. Even with his great birth-gift, he seemed powerless to change the situation. Her thoughts went to her brother. Thairyn had felt powerless too that day in the garden, and probably still did. She went to stand by her father and, putting her arms around him, wished for once she had her Aunt Nizza's birth-gift of giving comfort.

"Oh, Ardloh," Narrian sighed, moving to embrace him. Narrian was a tall, stately woman, but Ardloh stood taller. "You were always there for my parents, for my husband's parents and for all of us. You are more a part of en'Edlia than any of us. However will we manage without you?"

"I have been training my apprentice, Emija," Ardloh explained to all, drawing away from Narrian's hug. "She is highly capable and very talented. She will not believe she is ready, but she is. Be patient with her, Merrick. Her birth-gifts are strong. She has two, you know! She will be of great service to the high patriarchal family. It is her time now."

"Does she know you are leaving?" Merrick asked.

"Does anyone else know?" Narrian interjected.

"No, but I will tell her when it is time. No one knows but you, and I'd like to keep it that way until the new oracle is installed."

Phyre felt a heaviness in the room as the family sat already grieving the great oracle's passing over. She looked from one face to another, searching for hope, or a sign all would be well in spite of this sad news, but she found none. Her chest felt tight, and she tasted another salty tear.

"What about Emija?" Krystin asked. "Can she come to help us now?"

Ardloh shook his head. "Emija cannot act as oracle until she has been officially installed through ceremony. It will take some time to prepare."

"But what about—" Krystin began.

Ardloh stepped quickly to Krystin's side and took her hand. "Krystin, my dear, brave woman, I promise you all will be well with your son until Emija can be called into service."

Krystin's eye's looked moist again. "Thank you, Ardloh."

Merrick bent his head in sorrow. "I can't say goodbye to you, Ardloh. You have been my friend, confidant, and advisor since I was a boy. I have looked to you more than ever since my father passed over." He left Phyre's side to face the older man. "What shall I do without you?"

"You shall lead well, like your father and his father before. You shall hold your head up and do your best every day." Ardloh drew Merrick to him in a great embrace, and they wet each other's shoulders with their tears. "I shall miss you more than you know," the oracle whispered.

Phyre felt her own tears begin. She ran to bury her face in her mother's shoulder. Narrian again placed her arm around Krystin, drawing her close for comfort. "I wish Aunt Nizza was here," Jewl said, moving to sit next to her grandmother.

Ardloh finally coughed and straightened himself. "Enough of this blubbering! I have business to attend to." Phyre glanced up and saw Ardloh reach into his robes, and then hand her father a rolled parchment tied with green ribbon. "These are the instructions for the announcement and installation ceremony of the new oracle. It hasn't been performed in over two hundred years. See that you do it properly."

The high patriarch cleared his throat as he accepted the scroll, and then grandly bowed before Ardloh. "Yes, Great Oracle," he said formally.

"If you start that again, I shall jinx you from the great beyond!" Ardloh threatened.

Phyre gasped. "Would you really?"

Merrick had to chuckle, while Ardloh smiled and shook his head.

"I wish Nizza and the boys could be here," Narrian said sadly.

"So do I," confessed the oracle. "I don't have time to wait for their return, I'm afraid."

"When will you be leaving?" asked Narrian.

"Tomorrow at dawn. Will you give my best to the rest of en'Edlia?"

"Of course, but why don't you do it yourself?"

"Too many entanglements, too much time wasted," the oracle huffed. "And if you must know, I hate goodbyes!"

"I understand," Merrick replied quietly. "So I won't say goodbye either then, only farewell. Farewell, Ardloh, my friend, until we meet again." Merrick clasped Ardloh's hand tightly, not wanting to let him go as the rest of the family gathered around in a last embrace.

Phyre looked up at Ardloh and saw him gaze deeply into her father's eyes with great fondness. The oracle nodded his head, seemingly satisfied with what he saw, and vanished from the room, leaving an empty spot in their embrace that their hearts felt deeply.

Dragon Riders

CHAPTER 10

N aron stopped the wagon and looked over at Thairyn's sleeping form. They were nearing the village of Ner'ad. The boy had talked, eaten, and drunk a good deal of the way since Bay's Port. Finally, Thairyn had drifted off into silence, and then sleep.

Naron was uneasy with the memories of his own boyhood Thairyn had aroused. He had traveled with his parents, before their sudden deaths. It had been a happy time as he remembered. He wondered how his life would be now, if his parents still lived. He shook his head to rebury the tender feelings that had been uncovered. He must concentrate on the job at hand—retribution for his parent's death.

Naron woke Thairyn roughly. He inspected the boy's wrists and ankles. "There's sure to be questions about this," he said grimly, indicating the raw, red rope burns. "Tindus!" he called out, waking him as well. "Get the boy one of yer shirts. We don't need no nosy-bodies snooping around. "Roll up the sleeves a bit, but—"

"Now I'm a clothier!" Tindus complained. "Next ye'll be wanting me to measure the brat for a—"

"Shut yer yap, and do it!" Naron commanded.

Tindus pulled a worn gray shirt from his small duffle bag and pulled it over the boy's head. He rolled up the sleeves, leaving them long enough to cover the boy's wrists, and tugged the shirt down over the boy's tunic. "There, ye're happy now?" Tindus grumped.

"Do I have to wear this?" complained Thairyn. "It smells bad."

Ignoring both Tindus and the boy, Naron turned to Arth. "Keep the boy with ye while me and Tindus goes to get food and stuffs to get us to Dragon's Landing. Two more days and we should be on Claw Island. Then we can breathe easier."

Naron has a fleeting thought of a time when he and his father went fishing off an island. He had caught his first fish and had been so proud. Naron cursed. *Got to keep that boy out of my head!* he thought.

* * *

Ner'ad had come and gone without incident, so Naron was feeling good enough to let Thairyn ride next to him on the seat. Thairyn rode quietly at first, but then his curious questions bubbled to the surface.

"Why do you hate my family?" When he got no response from Naron, he continued his questions. "Why are we going to Claw Island? What's in Dragon's Landing? Will we see a dragon up close? I'm hungry. When can we eat? Can I walk with Arth for a while? Can we go fishing? I know how to fish, my father showed me. Do you know how to fish?"

Thairyn's barrage of questions began to grate on Naron. He had to keep a hard edge on his emotions. Naron's face looked like gravity was pulling on it harder and harder as each minute passed, until he was scowling, his brow deeply furrowed.

Abruptly, Naron reined in the hordle, nearly throwing Thairyn from the seat onto the creature's back. The boy's pants caught on a splintered board, which ripped a hole in the knee.

"Arth!" Naron bellowed. "Get this brat away from me, and shut him up before I put him back in the trunk and swallow the key meself!"

Jumping off the back of the wagon, Arth came, lifted Thairyn off the wagon, and set him on the ground. "Let's walk awhile," he said to Thairyn, glancing up at the angry face of their leader.

"Oh, boy!" cried Thairyn. "Thanks, Patriarch Naron," he called over his shoulder. He began to skip down the road ahead of Arth.

"Hang on to our money!" Naron yelled after them. *What on Irth was I thinking? Dealing with this boy is going to be me death fer sure,* Naron berated himself.

"Here, boy," called Arth. "Hold me hand. Don't want ye getting lost in this strange place."

Thairyn stopped and looked back at Arth. "All right," he answered, and waited for Arth to catch up to him. The too-long sleeves of the borrowed shirt were already beginning to unroll and were nearly dragging on the ground. Arth pushed up the one sleeve and took the boy's hand in his own.

They walked for several miles in front of the slowly plodding hordle and wagon. Thairyn asked Arth all his questions, while Arth patiently answered those he could. They chatted, smiled, and even laughed while swapping stories. Naron tried to ignore them both.

Naron watched the boy pick up several rocks and throw them over a bank toward the crashing waves far below. Thairyn stooped to pick more, and Arth joined him after rerolling the sleeves again. Arth's stone nearly hit the water, and Thairyn gazed on with admiration. "This is getting to be the best adventure I've ever had," Thairyn cried out.

More memories! Naron cursed himself. "Get going, ye two ruglumps!" Naron called as the wagon rattled by them.

Suddenly a shadow passed over them. Naron looked up quickly. "Dragon riders!" He cursed. "Run for cover! Now!" He slapped the hordle's back with the reins. It galloped forward, jolting Tindus into wakefulness in the wagon.

Arth paused a moment, scanning the skies. Then, he plucked up Thairyn and ran for a patch of sea pines just ahead. He pushed his way between two of the prickly trees and squatted, still clutching the boy.

"I want to see the dragon riders!" Thairyn told Arth as he struggled to get free.

Naron quickly drove the wagon into the brush and shadows near them. He leaped from the wagon. "Get undercover, bumphead!" he yelled at Tindus, who was still looking bewildered and half-asleep. "Dragon riders!"

Tindus fumbled out of the wagon, stumbling into the brush, just as a shadow chilled the air once more. Fortunately for the thieves, the riders were too high up to see much detail. However, the fact they were there indicated a threat Naron hadn't considered.

"We'll have to split up," he told the other men when they had maneuvered themselves together enough to talk. "Ye can be sure they're looking for the boy and us."

"What'll we do now? Tindus asked.

"Why are we hiding from the dragon riders?" Thairyn questioned Naron.

"Keep quiet or ye'll find yerself in the trunk!" Naron threw back.

Naron thought for several moments, and then said, "Tindus, ye travel only at night. Just move past the town and don't stop. We'll pick ye up on the road later. Arth, ye take the wagon and the boy. Get a room for the night and then in the morning, get the supplies we need for the island. Then, head on like ye're going to os'Uron. I'll go on alone to Dragon's Landing and wait for ye tomorrow beyond it. If anybody asks, ye're farmers from the other side of os'Uron, getting supplies for the cold season. Ask about where ye can get a boat to Claw Island. Say ye've heard the fishing is good there and yer wife wants—"

"Wife?" Arth exclaimed. "I haven't talked to me wife in—"

"Don't be a bumphead!" Naron said. "Ye're pretending, got it? The kid is yer son and ye're a farmer."

Tindus laughed. "Bumphead," he repeated degradingly.

"I got it," Arth said. "Me and Thairyn, we can be good pretenders, huh, boy?" He looked down at Thairyn. "It's like a game, see, boy. We get to pretend we're somebody else. Ye're already wearing yer costume. It'll be fun."

"That's right," Naron agreed sarcastically. "It'll be fun." He frowned, shaking his head. "Don't do anything stupid, Arth. Make sure we don't end up playing catch-me-if-you-can with the boy."

"Why not? That's my favorite game! I thought you said—" Thairyn burst out.

"Not that game! A pretending game!" Naron yelled at Thairyn. He took a breath, and then turned back to Arth. "Take it slow and easy. We got this far. Just play it safe and don't lose the little crown. Or else."

Arth nodded his head. "Sure, Naron. Whatever ye say. I'll take good care of the boy."

With a quick glance overhead, Naron took off at a run down the edge of the road, keeping to the shadows. Tindus made himself comfortable, waiting for nightfall. Arth lifted Thairyn back onto the wagon seat, and then took up the reins and climbed in himself. Arth slapped the reins, and the wagon lurched forward, slowly rattling over the dusty road toward Dragon's Landing.

The twins at the spy slit

CHAPTER 11

At the palace that very day, the second flying catlin arrived with more demands and instructions on the delivery of the ransom money. The thieves' message demanded the ruling family, or at least Krystin and her children, be exiled back to Earth, never again to set foot in en'Edlia. The twins listened anxiously while their father talked of splitting up the family and sending them to stay with their mother's family in Lyndell on Earth for safety. Krystin argued that she couldn't bear to leave one of her children behind and in peril. Merrick gave in, but doubled the guards.

Again, Jewl helped her father look into the catlin's memory to trace who had sent the ransom message. It had come from a different source than the first. It was a tavern on the other side of town near en'Edlia Bay's old wharfs, but no one could be recognized. The sender had taken great care not to show his face to the messenger before releasing it. Merrick sent guards there to bring in possible suspects.

The twins watched from a high palace window as Commander Arreshi brought in a prisoner encased in a force field generated by the commander's birth-gift. Jewl thought she wanted to be like Commander Arreshi when she grew up. The commander was strong and sure. She was smart and had a powerful birth-gift. Jewl knew she could not be that way. She would have to have people around her to draw power from. What good would she be then? They wouldn't need her.

Jewl refocused on the prisoner with the commander. It was the woman from the Shards. Jewl recognized her from her encounter with the catlin. Both girls knew they were not allowed in the interrogation room, especially with dangerous criminals.

"She doesn't look dangerous to me," Jewl protested.

"You know what mother would say," countered Phyre.

"Do you want to find out about our brother or not?" Jewl demanded.

"Yes, but—"

"Well, I'm going!" stated Jewl, and she started for the nearest go-betweens entrance.

Their Aunt Nizza had shown them the go-betweens barely a year ago. The go-betweens were secret passageways between the walls of certain rooms in the palace, installed for safe escape if under attack. They were also very handy for spying, should one choose to do so.

"I'm coming!" Phyre called. "I hope we don't get lost."

After descending several flights of stairs, slipping behind a hanging tapestry, and pushing through a moving wall panel, the twins were in the go-betweens. The go-betweens smelled dusty, and were dark, and full of purple, stringy seraph-spider webs. Holding up their fossi-shells the twins made their way toward the interrogation room. Their feet left prints in the dust, and they had to bat away the webs. Phyre edged around a golden spider fluttering its tiny wings as it descended trailing a purple strand. "I don't like this!" Phyre moaned, and then sneezed three times.

"Sssssssssh! We're almost there," Jewl whispered over her shoulder.

After a few twists and turns, the twins found their way through the narrow go-betweens to the spot behind the wall of the interrogation room. There was a spy-slit. However, the slit was too high for either of them to peer through.

"I have to see!" Jewl whispered. She thought for a moment, and then quickly tiptoed back down the go-betweens to a closer door that they had passed. She cautiously pushed open the door, grabbed the large pot that sat in the hall for decoration, and dragged it inside. She lugged it back to where Phyre stood, and silently set it underneath the spy slit.

They listened silently for a few seconds. Then, Jewl stood on the pot and slid back the spy slit. As she did so, they heard the commander's voice.

"Fhelda da'Jeria, do you understand you have been arrested for high treason against the realm of en'Edlia and the high patriarchal family? You will be sentenced to death if you don't cooperate in every way."

Jewl could see Fhelda seated with the force field shimmering around her. Fhelda had her head bowed. She looked nervous and frightened.

The captain repeated her question. "Do you understand the charges against you?"

"Yes, but—"

"The prisoner is yours to question, High Patriarch Merrick," Arreshi saluted, then stepped back, maintaining the force field around the woman.

"So you sent the catlin to the palace with the first ransom note?" Merrick questioned Fhelda.

"I didn't know anything about what the message was. The message was already in the delivery tube. I tried to find out, but the catlin wouldn't let me touch it."

"That's why you were chasing the animal?"

"Yes, I . . . how did you know that?"

Jewl looked at Phyre and nodded. She had seen it in the catlin's mind.

Their father continued his questioning.

"Then how did you come to send the ransom message? Do you know where my son is?"

Fhelda shook her head. "I don't know anything about a ransom or your son. My nephew gave the catlin to me three days before I sent it. How was I to know it had anything to do with a ransom?"

"Tell me everything you can about your nephew," Merrick continued.

The woman sighed wearily. "Naron's parents were accidentally killed when he was young and I, as his aunt, took him in. He was always such an angry child. He didn't understand why no one could revive the dead. I did the best I could with him but . . ." Fhelda paused at a sign from the high patriarch.

"I mean, what did he—Naron—tell you about the message, where he was going, anything which might give us a clue as to where he might have taken our son."

"That's just it. He wouldn't tell me anything."

"Weren't you suspicious because of that?"

"Of course, but I hadn't seen him in months. Nearly a year. What he does is his business, and I've learned to stay out of it."

"Then why did you agree to send the catlin if you weren't involved?"

"It was late. I was tired. Naron shoved the catlin at me and left."

"That's it?"

"I live alone. The animal provided some companionship for me. I welcomed the company. I tell you I have had nothing to do with Naron and whatever he is doing. You must believe me!"

"Is it true that your nephew is related to the Wizard Zarcon, who was exiled for high treason?"

"Yes, he was Naron's grandfather on his father's side, but they didn't—"

"We'll discuss that issue later," Merrick cut her off.

The girls waited anxiously while their father approached Fhelda and looked deeply into her eyes. He commanded her to remain still. Jewl could tell exactly what her father was doing. He was searching Fhelda's mind for more information and the images of people. He would determine if the woman was telling the truth.

"There!" Merrick whispered. "That's our man!" He broke contact with Fhelda. "Send in Rewl! Take the prisoner away. Hold her for further questioning."

Jewl knew that Rewl would be able to draw anyone her father had seen. Most likely it was this Naron that the woman had talked about. Phyre put her finger to her lips as the noise in the interrogation increased with movement of chairs and feet. Her face was pale with the stress of being there.

"Wait!" the twins heard Fhelda cry when the guards pulled her away. "I remember something."

"Well?" their father said impatiently.

"Naron took the old trunk with him. He was dressed all in black. He had a long traveling coat on and knee boots. Curse that boy! I swear I don't know any more!"

"Take the prisoner to her cell!" Arreshi ordered, handing off Fhelda to another guard.

Phyre recognized the sound of their father's pacing for a moment, and then he spoke quickly to Arreshi. "Commander, it was warm that night. If this Naron was dressed heavily, he must have been heading to sea. Find out who was on duty at the docks that night, and question them. See if they saw anyone matching his description, or carrying a large trunk, boarding any ship that night. Find out all you can, and report back to me immediately."

"Yes, High Patriarch!" the commander barked.

Jewl drew the spy-slit closed. "I wish I had father's birth-gift," she muttered as she leaned against the wall. Still the twins listened with their ears against the wall.

Heavy footsteps indicated someone was leaving the room. The door closed, then opened, and closed again.

"Ah, there you are, Rewl!" The girls heard their father's muffled voice again. "Let's get started on that drawing right now."

The twins knew Rewl well. Rewl was always called upon for criminal sketches, or family portraits, because his birth-gift made him particularly good at rendering faces. In a matter of hours, all of en'Edlia, and beyond, would be looking for Naron.

* * *

Skittering out of the go-betweens, the girls wandered off to the kitchens for a snack, and then slowly back to the patriarchal quarters. With their heads together, they whispered about what they had heard. As they came toward the entrance, they stopped just before the door. They could hear their parents' voices.

"It won't be long now," said their father.

"What about the second ransom note? It said if we didn't pay, they would k . . ." their mother couldn't speak the word.

"I don't care what they want," Merrick's voice rose in volume. "I'm not exiling my family because the Xens don't happen to like magicless off-worlders. They will pay for their crimes, I'll see to that."

There was the rustling of someone sliding on the satin sofa cushions. Then it was Merrick's voice again, but quieter. "We will find Thairyn and bring him safely home. I swear it!" Then, there were footsteps striding toward the door.

The twins barely had time to back down the hall so it didn't look like they had been eavesdropping, but were only just arriving.

Their father strode past them without a word, but then he stopped and turned. "Please be kind to your mother. She needs you to be strong now and help her. You'll do that won't you? Phyre? Jewl?" He looked at each of them in turn.

"Yes, Father," they chimed together.

CHAPTER 12

The grief of Phyre and Jewl's family had deepened at the news of Ardloh's departure and eventual passing over. Merrick had shown the family the scroll and made them promise to say nothing until the ceremony. His grief briefly turned to angry frustration. He cursed Ardloh's poor timing. However, the scroll's instructions were clear. They could not call upon the oracle's apprentice, Emija, for help until officially installed as Ardloh's replacement. The new oracle installation ceremony would take a few days to prepare for—possibly even longer, with the investigation proceedings of Thairyn's kidnapping taking priority.

The twins decided not to wait.

Phyre and Jewl had seen Emija at the palace many times during her apprenticeship. The girls had taken a special liking to her. The apprentice was gentler than Ardloh, who seemed gruff and intimidating most times. Emija was more like their Aunt Nizza— fun, playful, full of secrets, and even mysterious.

"Father said Ardloh was his friend and like part of the family, so it must be true about Emija too!" Jewl told her sister. The girls decided to secretly send a message by trusted servant to Emija that very day.

"What if Father finds out?" Phyre asked her sister as they huddled together in a corner of the music room.

"He won't," assured Jewl as she looked out on all the empty chairs and music stands. "Besides we're not asking Emija to do anything as the oracle. We are asking her as our friend."

"But what can we do? Father has already sent out the dragon riders, the country has notices everywhere, and all the commanders on the high council have gathered their forces to find our brother. What else can we do?"

"Something no one else has thought to do, of course!" stated Jewl. She got up and wandered around the room.

"What's that?" Phyre asked eagerly, following her sister with her eyes. "Jewl?"

Jewl turned slowly toward her twin. "I don't know. I haven't thought of it yet."

"Oh."

* * *

A message from Emija came back within an hour. The girls ran back to the music room to read it.

"Dear Phyre and Jewl,
Thank you for the invitation to come to the palace. Unfortunately, I will not be able to come just now. With Ardloh's leaving, I have many things to do, as you might well imagine. I will have to come tomorrow when things are more settled. Meet me at Sun's Apex in the west palace garden by the fountain benches for lunch.

Yours affectionately,
Emija."

Jewl angrily sat back, staring at the opposite wall, while Phyre looked sad. Suddenly, Jewl crumpled up the letter and threw it. "Why don't adults have time for us anymore? This is all Thairyn's fault!"

"How can you blame Thairyn for that?" Phyre asked. "He's just a child like us."

Jewl glanced over at her sister. "Because he got himself kidnapped, and now everyone is more concerned about him than us." Jewl folded her arms, daring Phyre to contradict her.

"But Emija said she'd come, just not today."

"I don't care," Jewl mumbled. "I just want this to be over."

"So do I, Jewl. So does everybody. But what can we do?"

"I don't know, but we have to think of something."

*   *   *

Emija came as promised the next day for lunch. Still dressed in her brown apprentice robes, she met the girls in the west garden very nearest the palace. The smell of flowers was heavy in the air and the sun, directly overhead, peeked through the clouds more often than not. It was a pleasant, grassy spot near a happily gurgling fountain. Phyre and Jewl looked like they belonged among the flowers in their long gowns of rose and fern-green.

Jewl watched Emija approach them. Even in her plain brown robes, Emija looked extraordinarily intelligent and lovely. Her gentle smile was warm and friendly, and her almond-shaped eyes shone with great power. Emija smiled at the twins as she seated herself on the carved wooden bench beside them.

"Well, what's all the mystery about?" Emija asked them. She set down her large basket packed with luscious fruits, sweet muffybread and mozer cheese.

"We need you, Emija!" cried Jewl looking into the apprentice's pale-green eyes. "Can't you find Thairyn?"

"Jewl, you know I cannot help as the oracle until after the installation ceremony."

"We're not asking you to do anything as the oracle, Emija," Phyre said quietly, taking a squirting sea plum from the apprentice's hand. "We're asking you to help as our friend."

"Oh, I see," Emija leaned over her basket, causing her shoulder-length blonde hair to fall forward to hide her smile.

Jewl looked at Phyre, who sadly shook her head.

"But why can't you help us?" Jewl jumped up and shouted. "You're just like all the rest! We get ignored while everyone is busy with more important things."

Emija's face came up quickly. She stared seriously at Jewl, who stood with her fists clenched and a deep frown on her face. Several seconds of stillness passed before the apprentice finally spoke.

"Jewl," Emija said softly, looking into Jewl's bright-blue eyes. "I can see into your mind. You are scared and worried about your brother, just as we all are. You feel helpless, and you don't like it."

"That's not fair!" Jewl protested.

"You are also jealous of the attention your brother gets."

"No, I'm not!" Jewl shot back, whirling around so that her long, dark braid swung out behind her.

"You asked for my help," Emija said firmly. "You must be honest with me."

"Can you help us then?" questioned Phyre hopefully, clutching her own braid in her hand.

"I'm not sure. Don't you think your father is doing all that can be done?"

"No," Jewl stated flatly. She turned and folded herself down onto the grass, sulking.

"What else do you think he should do?" Emija asked gently and then took a bite of cheese.

Jewl glanced up. "He can find Thairyn so things will get back to normal around here."

"He is doing all he can, I'm sure," Emija said, and offered them some bread.

"Which is why we asked you to help," Phyre explained as she brushed some crumbs off her green dress. "Isn't there something you can do that Father can't?"

"Your father has the whole of en'Edlia at his command. I'm sure he has thought of many things I could not have. He has more experience than I do."

"But you have great powers!" cried Jewl. "You're the oracle!"

"Not yet," the apprentice reminded her. "However . . ." Emija paused, twirling the tiny braid that hung by her right cheek.

The twins turned their full attention on the future oracle and held their breath.

"Yes?" they said together.

"However," Emija repeated, "I will try to do something to help."

Jewl leaped up from the grass, and both girls threw their arms around the young woman's neck and hugged her fiercely. "Thank you," they both cried.

When they finally released her, the apprentice said, "Now, can we eat our lunch? I'm starved!"

They all laughed then, settling into eating and making small talk. When they had finished eating, Jewl couldn't hold in her question any longer.

"But what will you do?" asked Jewl anxiously.

"I have an idea," Emija said smiling. "I'll let you know if I find out anything. And if I do discover something, you know I have to report it to your father."

"But what is it?" Jewl persisted.

"I'm not willing to say right now."

"Thank you for trying," Phyre said.

Emija stood and said her goodbyes. As they watched Emija walk away, Phyre turned to her sister. "Will we get in trouble if she reports anything to Father?"

"I don't know," Jewl replied, picking grass off her rose-colored dress. "But it's worth the risk."

Dragon Eggs

CHAPTER 13

As Thairyn and Arth traveled along, they discussed who they would be in their pretending. Arth insisted Thairyn call him "patria," which was slang for patriarch, and was a common name many children called their fathers. Thairyn had never called his own father "patria". It wasn't considered proper for the high patriarch to be addressed in such a common way.

Arth would introduce himself as Ekir, and Thairyn's new name would be Jonx. Once they decided, they began their charade immediately. Thairyn loved calling Arth patria. He tried his own new name out.

"I'm Jonx!" he said, waving to an imaginary person on the road. "This is my patria, and we are from east of os'Uron. We have a farm." Then he laughed and looked at Arth with a smile. "This is going to be fun!"

"Now, Thair—I mean, Jonx," Arth warned, "Don't be blabbing all ye know. That will seem strange. Only talk if ye are asked. Stay close to me. There be lots of strangers who travel through Dragon's Landing, and not all be friendly. I don't wish ye to get hurt or lost."

"All right, Patria," Thairyn sighed. Maybe it wouldn't be as fun as he thought. "Patria? What is your wife's name?"

"Why do you want to know?" the big man asked.

"Well, what if someone asks what my matria's name is?"

"Her name is Ennela."

"Ennela," Thairyn tried it out on his tongue. "I like that name."

"So do I," Arth replied quietly. "So do I."

"Do you have children? I mean besides me, of course." Thairyn grinned at Arth.

"Yes, four of them," Arth replied.

"What are their names?"

"There is me son, Chemail, and three daughters, Betheliza, Lanaia, and Eloreen.

Thairyn thought of Phyre and Jewl. "I wish I had a brother," he said aloud. He was lost in his own thoughts for a while, and then, another thought occurred to Thairyn.

"Do you think we will see a dragon in Dragon's Landing?"

"Most likely," Arth said, shrugging.

Thairyn jumped up yelling, "Great slimy sea slugs!"

Arth just shook his head. "Sit down and watch yer language," he said firmly, and then grinned.

"Yes, Patria," Thairyn said. He sat and smiled, too, as the hordle wagon rumbled and creaked down the road.

To Thairyn, it seemed to take forever to reach Dragon's Landing in the wagon. It was well after dark when he and Arth finally rumbled into the stable area at the edge of town. Along the way, Thairyn had succeeded in picking a much larger hole in the knee of his pants. He was stiff and sore from the long, bumpy, jostling ride on the hard, bench seat of the wagon.

After stabling the hordle and wagon, leaving the trunk still in the back, the pretend father and son made their way toward the Rhynstar Inn at Dragon's Landing. The Rhystar was a large, sturdily built, stone and mortar two-story structure. The thick, thatched roof covered great ceiling beams cut from the forests at et'Altere. The Rhynstar was in the center of town and seemed to be the hub of activity. Even though it was night, people still thronged the streets, many rode hordles or other beasts, some had wagons, while others, whose discussions were none too quiet, stood in small groups.

Torches and hanging fossi-shells lit the streets. The hard-packed dirt streets were wider than those in en'Edlia and, as they turned a corner, Thairyn soon saw why. Gasping and grabbing Arth by the coat, the boy suddenly stopped, unable to say anything but, "P . . . pa . . . patria!"

Ahead of them stood a full-sized dragon with a rider perched on its back. The rider was talking to a group of people just outside the Rhynstar Inn, but Thairyn had eyes only for the dragon.

It was a huge, emerald-green beast. Its head towered over the rooftops of the two-story buildings around it. It had two black horns that spiraled back from its crown and a back ridge of spikes longer than Thairyn's arm. Gleaming, smooth scales covered every inch of its lizard-like body. Its underside was slightly more yellow in color, and plated with wide, heavy, overlapping scales. With intelligence glinting in its bright, golden eyes, it took in every movement around it.

Thairyn was frozen with amazement and joy. He had seen dragons from a great distance, but had never seen one this close. He was transfixed with the creature's fluid motion and the sheer power it radiated. It was the most beautiful thing he had ever seen.

Letting out a roar, the emerald dragon stamped its enormous, talon-tipped feet. Thairyn nearly lost his balance as the ground shook with the impact. Then, the beast loosed a flicker of fire from between its long, shard-sharp teeth, and smoke rose from each nostril. The rider patted the dragon's neck soothingly, and quickly concluded his conversation.

At some unseen signal, the great dragon expanded its leathery wings and leaped into the air. Flapping with great pumps of its muscles, the dragon, with its rider, flew off into the night sky. In moments, they were out of sight in the darkness. Thairyn continued to stare into the sky long after they were gone.

Finally, Arth shook his shoulder. "Come, boy! We have to see about a room. It's getting late."

Overwhelmed by the crowds of unfamiliar people in the Rhynstar Inn, Thairyn was quiet and wide-eyed. Some people glanced his way, smiling or chuckling at the awestruck boy. The folk of po'Enay, giant, slender, dark-skinned people, and the short, pale-skinned, white-haired am'Orans were familiar as ambassadors to en'Edlia. However, the ones here seemed rough and uncivilized in comparison. Thairyn glanced down at his clothes and realized that in his too-big shirt and ripped, stained pants, he looked rough too.

Arth guided Thairyn through the crowd to the counter in the huge main hall, where they inquired about a room. The big-bellied man behind the counter gave a curt nod and motioned for them to follow him. The man, who was the inn keeper, led them through the gaming room, up a flight of stairs, and down a narrow hallway to a door marked with a red dragon. The keeper opened the door. Arth nodded and gave the keeper some coins. The keeper bowed slightly, gave Arth a small key, and then retreated down the hall.

Thairyn followed Arth into the small room. It smelled like oiled wood and sweet, dry grass. There was one low bed against the wall and a woven-reed sleeping pallet on the floor. A tiny table was pushed against the wall between the bed and pallet. On it was a rough towel, plain bowl, and pitcher of water. A fossi-shell hung on the wall and emitted a bluish glow, barely lighting the room. The room had no windows, and though sparely furnished, it was clean.

"This'll do fine," Arth said, looking over the room. He threw his own bag on the bed. Thairyn was just happy to be sleeping on something that wasn't moving for a change.

"Let's go get some food, then we'll get some sleep," Arth told Thairyn. "Got to get up early to get our supplies and be on our way."

"We get to eat?" Thairyn cried. "I'm starving!"

After locking their room, Thairyn and Arth hurried down stairs, through the gaming room, and into the huge main hall that was also the dining area. The dining hall was filled with heavy, wooden trestle tables and benches, which were crowded with people eating and talking. The room smelled smoky, spicy, and sweaty. At the far end of the room stood a great, stone fireplace built into the wall, its opening taller than Arth. The flames leaped over the wood that crackled and popped as it burned in the firebox. Above the fireplace was a massive, split-log mantle. Mounted above the mantle was the head of a beast Thairyn had never seen before; however, he was rather glad of that. It was a frightful thing, all spikes and fur, with glassy, orange eyes and wicked-looking fangs. Thairyn shivered at the sight of it, even though the room was overly warm with the fire and the crowd.

Curious about everything he saw, Thairyn tugged on Arth's loose-woven jacket and tried to ask him questions. Arth just shook his head, pushing him toward a table. Thairyn scooted around so he could sit facing the gaming room, rather than the beast over the mantle. All the activity fascinated him.

Soon, a skinny, young po'Enayan man came to take their order. He smiled broadly, his yellow eyes sparkling in the firelight, and his pointed ears fully exposed due to his very short, nearly-black hair. The server was so tall that Thairyn had to lean his head back as far as he could to see the man's face.

"Good morrow, friends," the server said. "How may I, Yonee, serve you?"

"Some stew and bread for me and me son," Arth said quietly.

"Your pleasure is mine," the waiter said, smiling. He spoke with a musical accent which made Thairyn smile, too.

Arth then asked about where they could purchase some supplies in the morning—food, bedding, cooking pots, fishing gear and such. The young waiter told Arth what he wanted to know and then hurried off toward the kitchen.

After the waiter left, Thairyn let out his curiosity. "Was he from po'Enay? How tall was he? I'm starving. Do you think we'll see more dragons? Wasn't that big, green one better than anything you've ever seen? What are they doing over there?"

Thairyn suddenly pointed to a table across the dining hall where several men sat around a table quietly, but intensely conversing. Some roundish objects lay in baskets on the table, which the men were hefting and inspecting from time to time.

Arth slapped down Thairyn's arm. "Don't do that!" Arth whispered harshly.

Thairyn gasped and hugged his arm as tears welled up in his eyes. Arth had never hit him before. "I want to go home," the boy cried in a low voice. He pulled up his knees to hide his face.

Arth's face softened. "Look, boy, ye can't be too careful in a place like this," Arth whispered. "We don't want no trouble here. If ye really want to know, those men are dragon-egg traders. They bring their eggs here to trade them with others or sell them to the highest bidder. The best dragon eggs are to be found right here, from what I've heard."

Thairyn raised his head. His eyes moved back toward the traders' table and the baskets of eggs. He felt his heart beating faster at the thought of just holding a dragon's egg.

"Don't get any ideas," Arth warned him. "Ye don't have any pa'trees to even begin to buy one of them. We don't want one either. Nothing but trouble, and we got enough of that already."

To cheer up the boy, Arth told Thairyn about the gaming room. "Not that we're going to spend any time there," he said firmly. Thairyn picked at the hole in his pants while Arth talked.

"There are many gambling games played on Irth. Some are played with shells and some with small, thin, wooden slats that are carved or burned with symbols, like the ones on the right there. See?" Arth nodded to the right. "Others use polished stones with several flat sides, each side being marked with a symbol or number. Other games are played with whatever the players have to bargain with, betting on or predicting an outcome of a play by others. Ye see, boy? These games are not for little ones," Arth finished.

Thairyn was just about to ask Arth if he could go watch, when the young server, Yonee, returned with their meal.

"Oh, and a mug of ale for me and some sweetwater for the boy, if ye please," Arth told Yonee.

"Your pleasure is mine," the waiter replied, and hurried away.

They heartily dug into the thick vegetable and meat stew. It was hot and savory with herbs. The taste was unfamiliar to Thairyn, but he liked it. The bread was dark and heavy, with a sweet, nutty taste.

Thairyn was hungry, but his attention was as much on his meal as it was on the dragon eggs. They caught the firelight like jewels! And the colors—emerald green, sapphire blue, gold, bronze, silvery pearl and ruby red! The colors seemed to swirl over their surfaces like oily liquid. Thairyn was entranced.

As Thairyn and Arth ate their stew, the egg traders got up to leave. One by one, they collected their wares into padded satchels or baskets and moved out of the dining hall. Many left the inn, while a few moved into the gaming room.

Thairyn watched them with longing eyes. His belly was fuller, but his hunger for an egg was growing. He didn't know exactly why he wanted one, but he had never wanted anything more in his life.

Thairyn nibbled his bread slowly, thinking all the while. People came and went in the dining hall, but he didn't pay attention to anything except where the eggs had been carried. Arth sat patiently sipping his drink and waiting for the boy to finish. The dining hall grew quieter as the gaming room grew noisier.

Finally, Arth stood. "Time to go, boy. Save yer dreams for sleeping."

Thairyn looked down at his leftover stew and sighed. He wished he had eaten it all. Now it was too late. He stuffed the remaining bread in his pocket and scooted off the bench. He still felt sore from the long day on the wagon's seat. His wrists and ankles still burned. With his belly full or nearly so, he was already becoming drowsy.

Arth moved through the gaming room close behind Thairyn. It was crowded, so they had to push their way through the people who gathered around the tables, cheering and bidding, laughing and cursing.

The press of people all around mesmerized Thairyn. He was jostled into one of the tables. Suddenly a flash caught his eye. There, right next to him, was an egg trader's basket so close he could see his own face mirrored on the bright surfaces of the eggs. Suddenly, there was a great shout across the room, and everyone stood or turned their heads to see what was happening. Everyone but Thairyn.

Time seemed to stand still while Thairyn gazed into the basket. A voice inside his head drowned out all other sound. *Take me!* it whispered. He felt his hand reaching up, closing around an egg of fiery red, and slipping it into his pocket with his bread. All at once, he was moving again at Arth's urging. The noise about him came crashing back to his senses. It happened in an instant. No one seemed to notice his theft in the wild scene of the gaming room and the moment's distraction.

Back in their upstairs room, Thairyn stood by the tiny table while Arth washed the boy's tear-smudged face and dirty hands. Then, he pulled the long, gray, borrowed shirt off the boy.

"Can't you just take me home now, Patria?" Thairyn asked quietly. "The others don't have to know. We can just slip away, and they won't catch us. We'll be good hiders." Thairyn looked longingly at Arth's big, tired face.

"Naron would never rest until he found and killed me, boy. Ye have to understand that about Naron. Nobody crosses him and lives."

"But, Father could protect you."

"No. That would be no life for me. There will have to be another way. Now be quiet and go to sleep."

A half-hour later, Thairyn lay on his sleeping pallet nibbling is bread and listening to Arth snore. He closed his hand around the dragon's egg he had hidden in his rough blanket. The egg was warm and comforting. He had wanted to tell Arth about it, but then couldn't. The egg was his. It just felt right. How was it no one noticed? How was it he had become a thief among thieves? Yet, he had never felt happier as he clutched the egg and then finally slept.

CHAPTER 14

As Thairyn slept, he dreamed of his family. He dreamed of playing with his sisters in the palace gardens . . .

Around the neatly trimmed hedges he raced, eluding the twins. Then suddenly, he was cornered, his sisters coming for him, their faces changing, looking frightening and unfamiliar. They grabbed him, tied him up, and put him in a sack. He struggled to get free. His heart was beating faster and faster.

Then, he felt himself growing, becoming too large for the sack. It ripped open under the strain of his growing bulk. He grew taller and covered with scales—red as rubies—as he towered over his captors. He felt wings burst from his shoulders. A deep fire kindled in his belly, while his fingers and toes sprouted long, sharp talons. His tail thrashed. His tail! He gazed down at himself. He was a great, red dragon!

Thairyn roared with glee. The strange twins screamed and ran away. He felt strong and powerful as he chased after them. His huge feet pounded the ground. He easily stepped over the hedges and crushed the flowers of the garden. The twins reached the palace, but Thairyn realized he didn't care about them anymore. He unfurled his wings, and in one, then two flaps, he was airborne. He flew away from the palace, banking toward en'Edlia Bay. He soared over the sea to Bay's Port, and then down the coast to Dragon's Landing. Circling, he looked for landing space. He touched down on the main street with an earthshaking thud, and let out a roar just to announce his presence. He felt so happy, so free, so strong and full of energy. The heat in his belly was bubbling up into his throat, so he opened his great mouth to let it out. Flames erupted from his jaws, charring half the building in front of him. Suddenly, Thairyn felt overly warm and getting warmer. He roared again and stomped the ground, trying to release the searing heat that was engulfing him . . .

All at once, Thairyn was awake. He sat up as the building trembled around him, and the roar of a dragon came from the street outside. He was sweating. The room was stuffy and something next to him in the blanket was very hot. Disoriented from his dream, Thairyn took several moments to remember where he was. His hand went to the hot spot, and he felt a lump. He reached into the blanket and pulled out the dragon's egg he had stolen. It was glowing red and extremely warm. It was too hot to hold for long. He dropped it on his sleeping pallet and stared at it.

It glistened like liquid rubies. Then, ever so slightly, it expanded in size. Thairyn double blinked. Had he imagined that? He looked up at Arth, who was still sleeping, and then back at the egg. Thairyn rubbed his eyes and looked again. He reached out, touching its surface. It was quite cool now. *Strange!* thought Thairyn. Maybe he had still been dreaming.

Arth stirred and yawned, rolling over on his bed. Thairyn quickly tucked the egg out of sight. Arth sat up. "Sleep well, boy?" he asked, yawning again. "We best be moving on. Get up, Jonx! Let's go." Arth threw the long, gray shirt at Thairyn and laughed when it landed on the boy's head.

*   *   *

Emija, the soon-to-be oracle of en'Edlia, slumped on her wooden chair in the small house she had shared with Ardloh. She missed him. The house seemed very empty without his large presence.

What do I do now? In just two days, I will be installed as the new oracle and be expected to fill Ardloh's place. The task seems impossible. I feel small and awkward compared to him. I'm not ready to be oracle!

She couldn't see herself storming into the high patriarch, giving him advice whether he wanted it or not, like Ardloh had done. Her voice was not loud or booming. It didn't instill fear or cause people to look up in awe.

However, two young girls had faith in her. They had asked for her help as their friend. How could she say no? She must do something, but what?

Emija stood and began to pace the room, which was both kitchen and sitting room. *Think, Emija!* she chided herself. Her pacing quickened. *Think!*

She thought back, remembering how Ardloh had handled certain situations. How he had made things right or guided others to make the right choice, find the right path, and discover things about themselves. She could hear his voice in her head.

"Emija, you are ready to take my place," he had said. She had started to object, but he cut her off. "I know you do not feel that way, but neither did I when my master, Wilcom, left me. I say to you what he said to me. All will be well! Trust in what you have learned, and trust in yourself. You have great gifts and privileges as an oracle. Use them. Rise to receive the respect that will be given you by virtue of your title. Live so as to be worthy of both the title and the respect."

His voice, gentle and loving, lingered in her mind. She clung to it. It reassured her. Her pacing slowed to a shuffle.

"Emija! Listen to me!" She heard Ardloh's voice again, clearly as though he were standing in the room with her. The force of it made her knees collapse. She plopped onto a chair.

"Ardloh!" she cried.

"Emija! This might be the last time I am able to speak to you. Though I am not there, I feel your fear and indecision. It grieves me. I feel weighed down by it. You must go forward. Believe in yourself. You are not me, nor are you expected to be me. Be yourself. Use your gifts. If you ever trusted in me, do so now, for I am telling you the truth. Be strong. All will be well."

"Ardloh!" Emija cried out again. Ardloh's voice faded, and then was gone. "Ardloh," Emija whispered. Then suddenly, she knew what she would do.

CHAPTER 15

Arth was quick to purchase supplies, load the wagon, and get back on the road heading south. Thairyn, not anxious to be sitting on the hard wagon bench again, stood in the back of the wagon with the supplies. It was just dawn, and they had been on the road for at least an hour already. Ahead, in the pale morning light, the road seemed to drop off the edge of a cliff toward the crashing sea below.

"Patria!" Thairyn cried, still using their pretend names. "Look at the road!"

"Yes, Jonx. Don't worry. The road makes a sharp turn to the east there, heading toward os'Uron and the City of the Lost."

"The City of the Lost?" exclaimed Thairyn. "Is that where we are going?"

"No."

"Then where?"

"Ye'll see soon enough, boy."

They continued down the rough, dirt road, bordered with sea pines and low coastal shrubs. Thairyn strained to see the turn, but the road dipped down slightly and was hidden from view. He wondered if Arth really was driving off the very edge of the cliff. He clambered over the back of the wagon seat and sat next to the big man for comfort. The road narrowed and became shadowy as the sea pines and brush grew closer on both sides. The morning air was cool, and all was quiet except for the constant rumbling of the sea and the creak of the wagon.

Suddenly, there was a harsh cry of a bird. Thairyn and Arth both looked up. Just then, two men leaped from the brush and grabbed the hordle's bridle, causing the animal to squeal and buck. The wagon rocked wildly, nearly throwing Thairyn out. Arth was quickly on the defensive, drawing his knife and leaping at the closest man. Thairyn yelled out as the second man ran toward him.

Arth's weight and motion took the one attacker to the ground, knocking the breath from him. "Stop, ye fool!" the man gasped. Arth's hand clutched the man's clothing, a knife at his throat. "It's me, ye big oaf!"

"Arth, it's Patriarch Naron!" Thairyn cried. Arth blinked, finally focusing on the face above his blade. "Naron!" Arth cried. He scrambled up, pulling Naron up with him.

"If ye've cut me, I'll take it out of yer share!" Naron touched his neck, cursing at the spot of blood that came away on his finger.

Arth drew back then, his own anger stirring. "Why did ye startle us like that? I could have killed ye!"

"You scared us!" Thairyn bravely called out as he stood in the wagon with his fists on his hips.

Naron dabbed at his wound with his handkerchief. A tense moment passed, and then Tindus burst out laughing. "Ye should charge him for the shave, Arth! And a close one too! Looks like he needs it," Tindus called out.

Indeed, none of the men had shaved since they left the ship, and their beards were darkening and filling in. "Ye bumphead!" Tindus laughed again. "Remind me to never ask ye for a shave!"

"Let's get moving before I decide to throw ye all to the razor fish!" Naron growled as he climbed into the driver's seat. "I want to be on the island afore dark."

"The island," breathed Thairyn. "What island?" he asked Naron, who took up the reins beside him.

"Don't talk to me, boy, unless I ask ye," Naron stated angrily. "Unless ye want to feel the back of me hand! I need to think."

Arth hoisted himself into the back of the wagon with Tindus, where the big man sat silently with his head in his hands for a long time.

Thairyn sat with his hand in his pocket, clutching his egg. He watched for the turn in the road, which came and went, and was miles behind them before anyone spoke again.

*   *   *

The thieves had been moving continuously closer to the sea as they traveled east. Finally, they were just a stone's throw away, and the land sloped gently down to the water's edge. It was late afternoon when the wagon finally stopped in front of a rickety, well-weathered, wood-slat building. It seemed to Thairyn that the building, which barely stood between the sea and the pines, would collapse in a mere breeze. It was bordered by some half-standing fences, which ran willy-nilly around behind it, but didn't seem to serve any purpose. The small animals in the yard wandered wherever they wished.

An ancient man sat on a wooden chair in front of the shack, his woven hat pulled low over his eyes, hiding most of his face. His gray beard, streaked with white, wandered down his chest, cascaded off at his waistline, and nearly brushed the ground. His hair and beard were entwined with all manner of twigs, moss, grass and others things, some of which were moving. His gnarled brown hands peacefully rested, folded over his beard.

Naron handed the reins to Tindus and jumped down from the wagon right at the old man's feet. The dust of the road made a cloud that drifted away. The man didn't even flinch.

"What's yer pleasure, young man?" a gravelly voice came up from under the tattered hat.

"We're looking for the boat master," Naron replied loudly as he looked around for someone else.

"Ye don't have no need to shout, sonny," the man replied. "Me hearin's jest fine."

"Then, do ye know where we can find the boat master, old man?"

"Yep. Sure do."

Naron stood waiting for the man to go on, but he fell silent.

"Can ye tell us where he is?" Naron asked loudly, becoming frustrated.

"Yep. Sure kin."

Again, Naron waited, but the man refused to say more.

Clenching his fists and his teeth, Naron kicked the bottom of the old man's outstretched boot. "Then tell us, ye worthless ruglump, before I stick ye in the gut!"

Slowly, the old man reached up and raised his hat above his eyes. Naron gasped and drew back. The others also stared. The man's eyes were bright purple rimmed in deep red. They had an intensity that could look into your soul.

"Ye . . . ye're . . ." stammered Naron.

"Yes, I am the boat master," the old man's voice was a piercing whisper. "And I know yer kind."

"Sir . . . I . . . I . . ." Naron continued to stumble upon his words as he trembled.

Thairyn was amazed at the sight of the old man and the effect he had upon Naron. He had never seen Naron afraid of anyone before. He almost felt sorry for Naron. Thairyn was curious too, for he felt no fear of the man with the purple eyes. In fact, Thairyn felt drawn to him. So, he climbed down off the wagon seat and came forward.

"Hello, patriarch," Thairyn began. "I'm sorry Naron was rude to you, but he's rude to everybody."

"Quiet, boy! Ye don't know . . ." Naron whispered.

The old man's eyes moved to take in the boy, and then his ancient face cracked into a small smile. "An innocent soul, but not quite," he said to no one in particular. "Come here, boy."

Thairyn walked quickly to the boat master and took his hand. "My name is Jonx," he said, remembering his pretending. "I am glad to meet you."

"I know who ye are," the master said. "I am a seer." Then he lowered his voice so only Thairyn could hear. "Ye will yet be great, but beware of these," he nodded toward Naron and Tindus.

"Yes, patriarch. Thank you," Thairyn whispered back.

The master smiled again and then reached out a bony finger to tap Thairyn's bulging pocket. "Be careful, me son, with this as well," he whispered. Thairyn's checks colored, and he looked down with guilt. "Do not worry. It was meant for ye," the seer confirmed with a wink.

Thairyn looked up and smiled broadly at the seer. *It was meant for me!* he thought.

"And now for ye," the seer looked up at Naron again. "Ye seek the boat master, and ye have found him. Do ye also seek a boat then?"

"Yes . . . yes, master," Naron replied. "We wish to go to Claw Island."

Arth nervously spoke up then, "Me and me son heard the fishing was good there, and me wife wants us to bring some herbs home for her."

"Do not speak of yer poor wife, Ennela, whose heart ye've broken," the seer answered sharply. "Or yer fatherless children, who cry for ye."

Arth gasped, and his face turned pale.

"Tell me no more lies!" the boat master hissed. He pointed toward the far side of the shack. ""There! There is yer boat! Take it, and go from me sight. Ye sicken me!"

The thieves all turned and looked where the seer pointed. There was a long rowboat and four oars leaning against the shack. Thairyn was sure it had not been there a moment before.

"But beware, and heed me words!" barked the old man as they looked toward the boat. "One of ye will never return this way, and one of ye will die."

Tindus chuckled, unafraid, "We all know who that will be," he whispered, looking in Thairyn's direction.

"And one of ye," the old seer continued, "will be changed forever."

The boat master pulled his hat down over his eyes once more. He crossed his arms over his beard and became still.

Naron stood frozen for a few seconds, and then silently motioned Tindus and Arth forward. They came warily, taking the boat with all the stealth of the thieves they were. Placing the boat in the wagon, they led the hordle slowly away, turning directly toward the sea on an overgrown path. Only Thairyn looked back and wished he could stay longer.

Seasick Thairgh

CHAPTER 16

Emija stood in her small house steadying her nerves. She glanced around at the wall shelves full of books and bottles and plants, both dried and living. She looked again at the map spread on the table in front of her. She wasn't sure how her idea would turn out.

The apprentice was among the very few on Irth who were considered as Ardloh's possible successor. Her gifts were not extraordinary, but the fact that she had two made her powerful indeed. Self-teleportation along with reading and controlling minds were her gifts. The reading of minds was often used, but the control was strictly forbidden unless death was eminent or permission was granted. Taking someone's freedom from them was a high crime, indeed. Teleportation of one's self took concentration and knowledge of the area. A simple jump to a location nearby was easy. Long distances took more energy, calculation and planning.

Ardloh had only let his apprentice wield the full measure of her powers on rare occasions so she could learn control. Yet, now Emija felt she had to know the limits of her powers. Better to try out the unknown on a friendly request and fail than bungle a high patriarchal command when it was crucial.

Ardloh had been strict in his training, demanding in his discipline, and exacting in the requirements of the use of magic. Now Emija would have to put those things together to test her abilities and stretch her confidence. She had come up with a plan which would require her to test her skills. She hoped it would also be helpful in finding young Thairyn.

Now Emija stood perfectly still—a feat in itself—willing herself to an exact point on the map she had just spent several minutes studying. Her concentration grew while she visualized the place she wished to be. She felt the dizzying sensation as her molecules began to vibrate in preparation for the physical jump through time and space. Suddenly, there was the disturbing feeling of being pulled, stretched, and sucked through a tiny hole, while surrounded by a swarm of zipperzulis all buzzing at once. Then, just when she thought she was going to be pulled apart, there was the sudden release, and she was free, flying through space. She could not see herself, but could sense the movement with every tingling nerve. However, the worst part, she knew, was yet to come. When she reached her destination, there would be a sudden stop, accompanied by the feeling of a trillion separate breakfast bugs hitting her skin followed by extreme nausea.

And here it comes—NOW!

Emija took a stumbling step and doubled over to lessen the sickening feeling as her molecules collected themselves at her new location. Ardloh had promised the last part would lessen as she used her gift more and more. The first time she had been violently ill for three days. Now it only lasted a minute or two, for which she was very grateful. She took a few deep breaths and then slowly looked up. If she had overshot, she might be in the middle of the Green Serpent Sea somewhere. If she hadn't pushed herself far enough, she might only be standing on the dock at en'Edlia Bay. She looked around. There was land in front of her, which was a good sign. The sea was at her back. Good.

Suddenly, a gust of wind blew her hair straight back and the ground shook. There was a mighty roar off to her right. *Perfect!* she thought. *I'm at Dragon's Landing.* All the leads to Thairyn's whereabouts had led to this side of the bay. This would be a good place to pick up more clues, if there were any to be found.

Emija strode forward with a smile on her face, feeling a bit more confident than she had a few moments ago. It was a long teleport, so she would need rest soon. Nevertheless, she had done it! Part One of her plan was complete.

*   *   *

The overgrown path led away from the boat master's shack. It ended at a small dock, where the long rowboat could be launched away from the rocky beach into the Green Serpent Sea. The island could be seen from shore, but it was a long row to reach the sandy Talon Beach, where the boat could be pulled up safely. The closest land on Claw Island was treacherous. It was called Draw-blood Point for good reason. The men would row toward the point, and then veer off to the right, skirting the rocky outcropping, to land at Talon Beach.

The men hefted the long boat with Arth on one side, and Tindus and Naron on the other. They grunted under its weight as they struggled with it from the wagon down onto the unsteady dock. Thairyn shuffled slowly through the tall grass, and then skipped down the dock. He was watching from behind and thinking how much this place smelled like home—the wet dock wood, the salty air, the green grass and trees. Something tugged at his heart as he looked out to sea.

"Out of the way, brat!" yelled Tindus as they swung the bow of the boat toward the end of the dock.

"Set it down! Set it down!" commanded Naron, between heavy breaths.

"Can I get in it now?" Thairyn asked, distracted from his thoughts.

"Can ye get in? What are ye—" Naron cried.

Arth cut in, "No, boy, not until she's in the water."

"She? Who's she?" Thairyn asked looking around.

"The brat knows nothing!" Tindus scoffed.

"She is the boat. All boats are called she," Arth explained.

"Why?" Thairyn asked. "Why do they have to be—"

"Enough jawing!" yelled Naron. "Let's heave her over the edge and get to rowing. The sun ain't going to wait on us." The men maneuvered the boat to the far edge of the dock. "Arth, hang onto the rope so we don't lose her."

Arth wrapped the towrope around a piling, and then prepared to push the craft off the dock. Tindus took up the front position on the opposite side, with Naron behind him. Thairyn began to count. "One . . . two . . . three!"

On three, Arth and Naron shoved the boat with all their might. Unfortunately, Tindus was fiercely hanging onto the boat, unready for the sudden thrust forward. The boat was successfully launched into the water, and so was Tindus. Now floundering, he cursed his misfortune, and blamed everyone else. The others all laughed as Tindus's water-matted head appeared above the edge of the boat.

Arth gave the unlucky, soaked-to-the-skin Tindus a hand up into the boat. They loaded their gear and pushed off with the oars.

"No time to change now, ye bloat fish!" Naron barked when Tindus reached for his bag. "Get to rowing!"

Arth and Tindus took up the oars and moved the boat steadily out to the deeper waters of the Green Serpent Sea. Naron sat at the stern, and Thairyn sat between the rowers. With the eastern breeze, the water was choppy, so the boat rocked and lurched unsteadily as the men drove the craft forward with steady pulls on the oars.

Thairyn had never been in a small boat on the open sea. After the first five minutes, his stomach began doing acrobatics he had never experienced before. The boy's face slowly turned the same grayish-green color as the water. "Arth, I don't feel so good," he moaned softly.

"Look to the horizon, boy, and face to the wind," Arth replied, pulling hard on the oars.

Thairyn glanced up to the horizon, then down at the rolling waves and dipping side of the boat. The sun was quickly lowering in the western sky. With the few clouds, it would be a glorious sunset on the water. However, Thairyn wasn't enjoying it. For the next ten minutes of the trip, Thairyn emptied the contents of his stomach over the side, dry-heaving the rest of the way.

Naron cursed the rest of them as he moved to the bow to escape the stench, sight and sounds the boy was making. "If I were superstitious at all," Naron yelled over the wind, "I'd put to shore right now and abandon the lot o' ye!" Thairyn hoped he would do just that.

It was an hour's hard row from the dock to Draw-blood Point. There, Naron took the oars from Arth. "See to the boy," growled Naron. Tindus insisted on rowing. His long-sleeved striped shirt and blue, rough linen pants were drier, but the sweat from rowing kept them damp in places.

The water's push to the shore of the island aided the next half hour's rowing. Weary and wet, they finally landed on Talon Beach. Of course, since Tindus was still wet, he was elected, or rather thrown cursing over the side, to haul the boat closer in, so no one else had to get soaked in the process.

Arth clambered out of the boat, leaping over the surf to the sandy beach. Then, he took the towrope from Tindus and pulled the craft completely out of the water. He hauled Thairyn, limp as seaweed, and nearly the same color, out of the boat and laid him gently on the beach. Naron threw the gear out onto the sand and climbed out of the boat, while the angry, dripping Tindus slogged up the beach to find a dry spot. Lastly, Arth dragged the craft further inland, tying it to a huge driftwood log well above the tide's reach.

"Turn 'er belly up! Storm's brewing," yelled Naron. Arth turned the boat upside-down to keep out the rain.

Too tired to hike inland, and with the sun's light nearly gone, the small group camped on the beach. A fire was built with driftwood, a simple meal prepared, and bedrolls were laid out on the sand. The point's curved, rocky outcroppings gave them protection from the east wind.

Tindus stripped himself of his wet clothes and laid them to dry. He snatched back his gray shirt from Thairyn. "I'll be needing that more than ye, brat." Tindus pulled it on, and then gasped. "And ye said it smelled bad when I gave it to ye! UGH!" Thairyn was frankly glad to be rid of it.

If he hadn't still been seasick, Thairyn would have been dancing with excitement at the whole prospect of camping on an island. He lay in his bedroll, still feeling the pitch and roll of the waves, and moaning much of the night. "I'm never getting in that boat again!" he muttered.

Naron glanced at the boy and grinned. "I'm going to sleep well tonight!" he told Tindus. "No worrying about the little crown wanting to row away on his own any time soon."

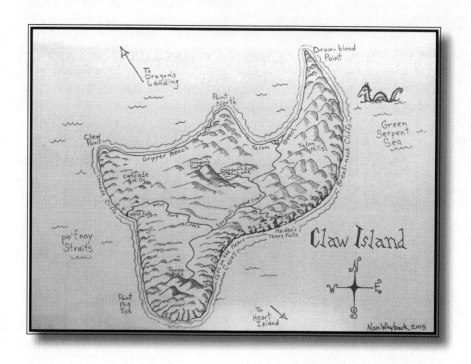

CHAPTER 17

The morning was cool and foggy. Everything felt damp and gritty with sand. The air smelled sharply of brine and seaweed. Naron was up first, rousting everyone else to break camp and get moving. "We've a long hike ahead of us, so get a move on!"

Thairyn felt empty and weak. He hadn't slept well, and one look at the soupy fish chowder Arth had cooked made his belly lurch. He'd go without rather than risk losing it all later in another bout of sickness. He still felt light-headed and shivered in the cool dampness of the morning. Arth gave him a few sips of water to cool his throat and ease the griping in his stomach.

"Come on, boy," Arth called to him. "Some fresh air and walking will clear yer head."

They shouldered the packs, filled with the provisions Arth had purchased at Dragon's Landing, and headed away from the sandy beach. The island was rocky and hilly— not a flat place to be seen beyond the beach. They followed Serpent's Tongue Creek inland to the southwest.

After walking awhile, Thairyn did begin to feel better. He started looking around and noticing his surroundings. They followed the rocky creek into the low hills dotted with sea pines. The ground was mostly rocky. Large boulders nudged up next to smaller piles of dark brown or rust-colored rocks and those were surrounded with a variety of pebbles and rocky soil. In between the rocks, grew low, leafy shrubs, grasses, and bushes, some with bright orange berries or tiny white flowers. Thairyn wondered if the berries were edible. He plucked up a few, sniffed them, and rolled them around in his hand. The berries were round and had a bitter smell.

"Got a death wish, brat?" Tindus sneered. "Go ahead and eat some." He laughed. "Then Naron won't have to kill ye himself."

"Arth?" Thairyn frowned, turning toward the big man, the berries still in his hand.

"It's true, boy," Arth replied. "They are deadly poison until they turn yellow. Then ye can eat them, but I wouldn't."

"Why?"

"They taste like mozer droppings," Arth said, smiling.

Tindus laughed again. "And ye'd know just how that tastes, wouldn't ye, bumphead?"

"Quit jawing and keep walking!" Naron yelled from up the trail.

Tindus quickened his pace up the path, leaving Arth and Thairyn bringing up the rear. After trudging along for over an hour, Thairyn noticed a larger peak to the right rising above the hills.

"Are we going there?" Thairyn asked Arth, pointing to the small mountain.

"That is the Dragon's Tooth. Right below it, is Dragon's Eye Lake. I wish we were going there."

"Why?" Thairyn asked again.

"Because it is very beautiful there, with the mountain's reflection in the lake. Lots of fish and fresh water. Even a small island deer or two for game."

"Where are we going then?" Thairyn asked.

"Only Naron knows for sure, but it is definitely beyond the Dragon's Tooth."

In two more hours, the Dragon's Tooth was behind them. After much complaining from the group, Naron finally called a halt in order to eat and rest. Thairyn gratefully let his pack slide off his shoulders and plopped down on a flat rock. The creek offered them fresh water, and they pulled dried meat and fruit from the packs.

"It's not far now," Naron told them. "We'll cut left at the next stream and head for the east coast. There are caves there we can hole up in."

"How long are we going to stay there?" Thairyn asked Naron.

"For the rest of yer life, little crown," Naron's mouth smiled, but his eyes looked cruel. "For the rest of yer life."

The embryo reveals Thairyn's face to Emija

CHAPTER 18

Emija walked the busy streets of Dragon's Landing asking those she met if they had seen the boy, Thairyn. She gave them a description of the boy and Naron. She was careful not to reveal the true identity of the boy. No one in the diverse group she encountered seemed eager to talk with her or give her any information. Mostly their answers were uncommitted shrugs or head shaking.

Finally, she went into the Rhynstar Inn to sit, think, and rest. After Emija had seated herself at a long trestle table in the eating hall, a tall, young man came to wait on her. His yellow eyes, dark skin, and pointed ears set him apart as po'Enayan.

"Good morrow, apprentice. How can I, Yonee, serve you?" he asked pleasantly.

Emija was surprised that he recognized her, but then she remembered all apprentices wore the simple brown robes like hers. She smiled up at the server, wanting to remain unknown for the time being. "I would like a small bowl of soup and some bread, please."

"Your pleasure is mine," the server replied. He smiled and scurried off to the kitchen.

When the young man returned, and bent low over her table to serve her food, Emija quietly spoke to him. "In the last few days, have you seen a young boy here, about seven years old, accompanied by three men? They overpaid my master for a service," she lied, "and I have been sent to return the overpayment to them. I was told they came this way."

"There was a young boy here yesterday," the server said. "Or was that two days ago? So many people come and go around here." He stopped and smiled. "But not many children here, as you may understand."

Emija nodded to Yonee, the server, and then described Thairyn to him. He raised his hand to his chin in thought.

"Sounds like the boy, but he was with his father alone," he replied.

Emija looked puzzled. "His father? What did he look like?"

"He was a big man, not as tall as me, but large." Yonee motioned outward with his hands and arms. "Looked like a farmer or worker of some kind. Hair about your color, dark eyes."

"He might be the one I seek," replied Emija. "Did he say where they were headed?"

"No, but he did ask where to buy supplies and bed rolls. Might have been going east toward os'Uron. Fishing is good now along the coast. Some of the inlanders come for several days before the seas get too rough."

"Thank you for your help, Yonee. Do you have a place in town where you keep official notices from the high council?"

"Yes, right here at the Rhynstar," he replied proudly, pointing towards one of the game room walls. "If you have something to post, you will have to ask the owner."

"Just like to keep updated on what's going on. Thank you again." Emija ended the conversation and began eating.

"Your pleasure is mine," said the po'Enayan as he moved away to another table.

Emija sat thinking. The description of the boy's father didn't match the description of Naron. Could it be they had split up? Or were the other two elsewhere at the time? Emija wondered if the notice posters of Thairyn's kidnapping had been put up here. Surely, someone would have noticed it, along with the oddity of a young boy here in Dragon's Landing, and put the two together. She would check when she finished eating.

Now she took her time to look over the others in the place and gather what information she could by observation, listening, and even a little mind reading. She tried not to invade people's privacy, but sometimes, as Ardloh would say, the breakfast bug's in the batter.

The apprentice oracle let her mind reach out into the room slowly and gently. She touched conscious minds of many different races here, but there was something else. Oh, it was the dragons, of course. Their keen intelligence was felt on a an emotional level rather than as word-thoughts. Her mind reached out further, touching other's surfacing thoughts, which were easy to access without any notice on their part.

The man at the end table was worried about the coming growing season. His companion agreed, but was more concerned about his own problems. A pair of am'Orans was trading old sea stories in the other corner. Four men sat bartering their wares, each one thinking he was getting the best deal. The young man, Yonee, was thinking about a certain pretty girl he was meeting after work.

Not much useful information there, thought Emija sadly. She stretched her mind into the gaming room. Such a wild range of thought here—intense plotting to win a game; dull, uninterested mind drifting; even some giddy anticipation of winning with the payoff. Still no help.

Suddenly, a strange little niggling brushed against Emija's consciousness.

Emija withdrew slightly. She was taken off guard by this unfamiliar touch. She cautiously extended her mind out again, gently brushing up against the niggle. It was a happy, expectant niggle— almost a tingling, like compressed excitement on the verge of exploding. Where was it coming from?

Emija withdrew again. She would have to press deeper. Did she dare? Many unknowns, seemingly innocent at first, could prove to be dangerous. She couldn't afford to become entangled in something now when her installation as oracle was tomorrow.

Tomorrow! That thought made her heart leap. She would need time to rest and get ready. She needed to finish here quickly and return to en'Edlia. *Perhaps I will just go see what I can find in the gaming room, check to see if Thairyn's poster is there, and ask the owner if he can tell me anything,* she thought. She popped the last morsel of bread into her mouth.

Leaving a modest tip for the server, she headed for the gaming room. It was crowded, even though it was still daylight. Most places like this were deserted until evening but, she reasoned, what else is there to do here if you aren't dealing in dragons?

The gaming tables were busy, and the noise intensified as she came nearer. There was nothing new here. They played some of the same games in en'Edlia and po'Enay. The games she didn't recognize were being played mostly by those from the Raden Islands. Emija had never been there. The trade between their countries was still in its early years.

The apprentice pushed deeper into the room, touching the minds of those around her in passing. She spied the poster wall to the left and moved toward it. She shook her head as she neared it. No wonder no one here had noticed the royal decree about the young crown patriarch's kidnapping!

Emija stood before a wall plastered with posters from all over Irth. It was impossible to tell where one notice ended and the next poster began. There was one on top of another, on top of another. Emija wondered how thick this wall of posters might actually be. The decree was most likely there, but buried under many others received in the last several days.

Then, there it was again—the niggle. She moved toward it physically, trying to glimpse what it might be, but she stopped when it drew her into a dark corner of the room where two men sat.

Emija turned away, and found a place nearby where she could sit without much notice. She looked at the two men in earnest discussion as they pushed a basket back and forth between them. *Such odd behavior,* Emija though. Then it became clear when one of the men drew out a roundish object from the basket, pointing decidedly at it.

Even in the shadows of the corner, the dragon's egg caught the light with a quick but elegant flash of sapphire blue. Emija gasped at the revelation. Now she no longer feared the niggle. It was the searching of an embryo for its bond mate. She sent her mind out willingly to touch it, to tickle it ever so gently. The niggle responded with joy, and then sadness.

You are not the one.

Emija felt a slight pushing away of her mind, a rejection of sorts. *I know. My path lies in a different way,* she thought back.

What of my companion?

Emija then sensed a second egg still lying in the basket. She tickled it too. There was little joy from this one, only longing.

It has lost its last clutch-mate and longs for The One to find it, the first explained.

Intrigued, Emija pressed deeper into the second egg. As she did this, all sound faded away. It seemed there were only she and this tender embryo in the entire universe. She felt its color—red, deep as a blood-ruby. She felt its longing, which nearly broke her heart. Then she felt its mind, like the brush of a new leaf in a spring breeze.

You are not the one, the red embryo projected to the apprentice.

My path takes me another way, but can I see? There was an anxious pause.

Will it hurt?

No.

Then, yes, come closer.

Emija let her mind sink deeper into the consciousness of the red dragon egg. It was like watching or feeling slow motion scenes from the embryo's perspective—a replay of the embryo's emotional experience. Emija viewed what the embryo had seen and felt. She saw a hand reaching toward it, brushing it, and then taking the red egg next to it. Then she saw that hand withdrawing with the egg disappearing as the hand put it into a pocket. The feelings of longing intensified the farther apart the eggs became—a terrible ache that could not be consoled. A loneliness that was overwhelming.

Emija began to withdraw, the intensity of the emotions surrounded her, she had to pull away. Suddenly she stopped. There in the embryo's memory was an image of Thairyn! She had missed it at first. Reflected on the egg's gleaming surface was a skewed image of the young crown patriarch. There was no doubt. Hope leapt higher in Emija's soul.

Expressing her hope for the embryo's future, she quickly conveyed to the embryo what it had done for her and all of en'Edlia, and gave it the emotional equivalent of a hug and kiss. *You must be truly a wonder indeed to have accomplished such a great feat while still unborn and unclaimed. Pure magnificence!* she told it.

As Emija withdrew completely, she felt satisfaction and peace replacing some of the embryo's longing. That made her smile.

The setting sun sent a ray through the window glass directly at the apprentice as if giving her a signal it was time to return to en'Edlia.

I have what I need. Emija thought as she rose from her seat and headed for the door. And perhaps she did have what she needed to be an oracle as well.

Maiden's
Tears Falls

CHAPTER 19

"Welcome home, me lovelies!" Naron dropped his pack at the entrance of a cave. Arth and Thairyn had caught up and were coming into the cave as well.

"Why this one? Why not one of the other twenty or more we already passed?" Tindus complained.

"I scouted these caves personally to find the best one, and this is it, sponge-for-brains! Take it or leave it," retorted Naron.

"If ye ask me—"

"I didn't," Naron stopped him. "Now unpack and settle in. I'm leaving in the morning again."

"What? Leaving again?" Tindus spouted off. "You—"

"Got to attend to a few more important details," Naron cut him off.

"And how do we know one of those important details isn't picking up the ransom and never coming back again?" Tindus questioned the leader.

Naron walked slowly up to Tindus, his eyes never leaving him. He put his hand on the smaller man's shoulder in a somewhat friendly gesture, but still Tindus flinched.

"Tindus, I never thought ye had much brain, but now ye've changed me mind! I never thought of that little plan ye just mentioned there, but I like it. I like it a lot."

"Thanks, Naron," Tindus replied shyly. "I thought it was a good one . . . but—wait!"

Naron slapped Tindus hard on the back, knocking him forward a couple stumbling steps. "Don't worry, ye sea wart, I'll not leave ye stranded on the island long." Naron laughed, and then walked off to his pack, leaving Tindus to muddle over what just happened.

Thairyn dropped his pack on the cave's sandy floor and began to explore. The mouth of the cave faced southeast, out toward the Green Serpent Sea, on the narrow strait between Claw and Heartbreak islands. The east wind whistled through the cave entrance, bringing with it the smell of the open sea. Fortunately, the entrance was shallow, the hollow turning to the right, and then opening wider into a larger cave. The cave ceiling was high enough even Arth could stand upright inside. There was room to spread out, so each had a space. Naron had brought fossi-shells, which he put in niches in the rock walls. The food was placed high on a natural rock ledge on the left side of the cave. It was well beyond the reach of wild animals and Thairyn as well. A tiny cave nearby would be used as a bathroom. Arth called it the 'leavings' cave, because they were leaving something there they would never take away. Thairyn was glad of that.

Then, Thairyn heard water bubbling. He saw a small pool to the left, the water gurgling up at its center. The water was so clear, that the pool would have looked empty except for the constant movement of the small spring. This would be their source of fresh water. The spring overflowed and formed a streamlet, which snaked its way out of the cave entrance, twisting and turning over the rocky ground.

Thairyn followed the water's course with curiosity into the cave and back out. Tracing its winding course, he saw many other streams join it, until it finally plunged over the edge of the steep, island cliff side into the sea. Thairyn stood on the cliff's edge gazing at the cascade of water. A moment later, he felt a hand on his shoulder as Arth came up next to him. "Careful, boy," the big man said quietly.

"Where does the water go?" asked Thairyn.

"It joins the sea far below. Sailors call these falls the Maiden's Tears." Arth pointed away to the left.

Thairyn looked and saw other small cascades of water. "Who is the maiden?"

Arth chuckled. "Have ye never heard the story of the King of the Sea Trolls?"

Thairyn wrinkled his nose and stuck out his tongue. "That's a girl's story, with all that love stuff!"

"Someday ye'll be more interested in all that love stuff," Arth laughed. "That is the maiden who still cries for her lost love."

"Sea slugs! I bet my sisters wish they could see this!" Thairyn smiled, then slowly his smile faded, and he sighed. He realized he hadn't thought about his family for a while, or the fact he was kidnapped. His kidnapping had become more of an adventure he was enjoying. "Arth, what's going to happen to me?"

Arth hung his head, shaking it. "Nothing if I can help it," he replied wearily.

"But what if you can't help it? What if you can't, Arth? Then what?"

Arth was silent for a while as he looked out to sea. "Time to go back now, boy," he said finally, steering Thairyn away from the cliff's edge.

Thairyn is caught with the egg

CHAPTER 20

Naron had been wise to leave the island early. The late morning had turned cold and wet with a brisk wind coming off the Green Serpent Sea. The east wind swept over the land, commanding all to bow and shudder at its very presence. The island was shrouded with fog, which the wind seemed unable to clear away, or perhaps there was just no end to it. Rain poured down, saturating everything, the wind driving it into every crevice.

Gathering wood outside the cave, Tindus was angry. He was angry that he hadn't thought to collect more wood before the rain. He was angry because, once again, Naron had disappeared on some unknown business, leaving him with the brat. He was angry at the damp, cold place they had to stay, and the meager rations they had to eat. He was angry with Arth for taking the boy's side in nearly every argument. He was angry that he was wet again in the rain. Everything about his current situation made him angry. He hated it all.

Shivering, Tindus returned to the cave with his armload of wood. He threw it down, and stood with drops of rain dripping off his bushy eyebrows, long, pointed nose, and the tip of his grayed, scruffy beard. Then, he glanced up at Thairyn, who was kneeling on his bedroll. The boy had a strange look on his face, a mix of terror and guilt. Instantly suspicious, Tindus looked more carefully at the boy. Then, he spied a sparkle of red between the boy's clutched fingers.

"What ye got there, brat?" Tindus questioned him. "Found a treasure?"

Tindus moved closer to where Thairyn knelt next to the cave wall. The boy turned away and tried to cover whatever he held. Tindus rushed forward and grabbed the boy up by the hair, while Thairyn struggled to conceal something.

"Give it here, brat!" Tindus yelled, shaking him by the hair. Thairyn cried out in pain. Tindus threw the boy down and pounced upon him. He grabbed the boy's hands and pried them apart.

"No!" Thairyn wailed. "No, it's mine!"

The boy was no match for the wiry man, who painfully forced his smaller fingers open. Tindus scooped up the boy's treasure and danced over to the other side of the fire.

"Now we'll see what ye are hiding from me, brat. Ye wants it? Do ye?" Tindus pranced back and forth, taunting the boy. "Come get it then, brat," he coaxed holding out his closed fist.

Thairyn got up and moved toward the man. He held out his hand. "Give it back," the boy cried. "Please!"

"Oh, now it's 'please' is it?" Tindus jerked his hand back to his chest. "Let's just see what yer so worked up about." Tindus opened his fist and stared at the roundish object in his hand. He turned it over and over. Then, he held it up to the firelight, his face bunched up as he tried to examine it. "That's it? A rock?" hollered Tindus. "All that fuss over a rock? I thought I saw . . ."

The boy's mouth fell open. He stared at the rock Tindus held up. It was the same size and shape as the dragon egg, but it was dull, gray, and rough—looking very much like an ordinary stone.

Tindus stared at the rock in his hand then back at the boy. He saw increasing panic come over the boy's face, but didn't understand why. "Ye wouldn't be hiding something else, now would ye?"

Thairyn shook his head, his eyes fixed on the stone.

"We'll just see about that!" Tindus ran to Thairyn's bedroll, yanked it up, and shook it. Nothing but sand spilled out. Tindus backed Thairyn into the cave wall. "Why were ye hiding this? Trying to make me look stupid, brat? What's so special about this rock? Yer mama give it to ye?" Tindus laughed cruelly and walked away from Thairyn. "Ye want it? Come get it!" he dared Thairyn.

The boy edged closer to the man, his eyes staring at the rock. At the last moment, Tindus pulled the rock away, laughing. He turned toward the mouth of the cave. "Ye want it? Go find it!" and he made to throw it outside.

Thairyn cried out, just as Arth loomed in the cave entrance, blotting out the meager daylight. Both the men's shadows fell over Thairyn. "What's going on?" The big man looked menacingly at Tindus.

Tindus pulled up short, the rock still in his hand. "We was just playing a little game of hide the rock, weren't we, brat?" He tossed the rock into the air and caught it.

"He won't give it back," accused Thairyn.

"What's the big deal about a stupid rock anyway?" Tindus griped. He turned toward the boy with malice on his face.

"Give the boy his rock," Arth said with a sigh. "It's just a rock, Tindus."

"Fine! Ye want yer precious rock? Here ye go," Tindus held the rock out, walking around the edge of the fire. The boy's eyes were wide, watching the man's approach. Thairyn held out his hands expectantly.

Tindus meandered around the fire pit, taking his time. Arth was busy setting down his gathered wood, then wrestling himself out of his soggy overcoat. The big man drove a heavy stick into the sandy ground and hung his coat on it to dry. Then, he cozied up to the fire, poking and feeding it to intensify the heat.

Finally, Tindus stood close enough to the boy to hand him the rock. "Ye want this rock?" he taunted. "Can't sleep without it? Poor baby!"

Arth looked up, frowning. "Just give it to him."

Tindus smiled an evil smile. He turned slightly and flipped the rock intentionally into the fire pit. "Oops! Oh, bottom-spiders! I dropped it!" the man cried out innocently.

The boy gasped and dove for the fire, stopping just short of plunging himself into the flames.

"It's all yers, brat! Get it if ye can." Tindus sauntered off to the other side of the fire and sat down to warm and dry himself. He glanced at the boy to see his reaction.

Thairyn stood up, a deep scowl on his young face. He slowly clenched his fists and his whole body began to shake. The boy's breathing quickened, and his green eyes filled with hatred.

Suddenly, Thairyn charged Tindus. The boy threw himself upon the man. The boy screamed, kicked and pounded on the man with all his might. Tindus was overwhelmed by the unexpected ferocity of the boy's attack. He tried to thrust the boy away from him, but Thairyn continued to pummel him relentlessly. *The boy must have gone mad,* thought Tindus.

"Arth! Get this wildcat off me!" Tindus cried.

"Thairyn! Stop!" ordered Arth. "Stop, boy!" Arth stood up, reaching for the boy.

Tindus pushed the boy away again. "I'll not be bested by a breakfast bug!"

Thairyn screamed and charged Tindus again. This time the man jumped up and backhanded the boy hard in the face, knocking him to the ground.

Thairyn lay on the sand. His eyes closed and his chest heaving. Tears were pouring down his check where a nasty bruise was beginning to show.

"Ye little brat!" Tindus spat blood from his mouth, where Thairyn's fist had made contact.

"I hate you!" screamed Thairyn. He clumsily got to his feet.

"I'll teach ye like me patria taught me," Tindus cried. "I'll beat ye till ye can't move no more!" Tindus swore. The boy flung himself again at Tindus, but Arth rushed forward and caught Thairyn in his arms.

"Let me go!" Thairyn yelled through his tears. "I hate him! Let me go!"

Arth held Thairyn while he continued to rage and cry. Tindus yelled and cursed, but kept his distance from Thairyn. He was spooked by the boy's attack. Tindus didn't have much experience with children, and he had pushed his own miserable childhood deep into the far corners of his memories. *The ransom better be paid and soon,* he thought. *I didn't bargain for this. Naron owes me plenty.*

"Let it go, boy," Arth said, trying to comfort Thairyn. Finally, the boy reached the point of total exhaustion, and could do nothing but silently cry.

"I think the brat's gone mad! You keep him away from me," Tindus said, pointing a shaky finger at Thairyn. "We'll all be mad afore this is over. Mark me words!" Tindus stalked off deeper into the cave to settle his nerves and sort out his feelings that had suddenly turned colder and more bitter.

*　*　*

Later that night, Thairyn awoke in a heap in his bedroll. Now the cave was dark. The men were snoring. The fire had died down to glowing embers. Thairyn couldn't sleep. Something had snapped and broken within him before he had attacked Tindus. Thairyn felt defeated, empty, and hurt. He touched his check and winced at its tenderness. He had been careless, and now this was the consequence. He had lost the only thing that had been truly his and his alone. He had lost the dragon's egg. He had even searched through his bedding and the sand in case it was just a rock, but he knew somehow exactly where the egg was even if it didn't look the same. He was sure the unborn hatchling was roasted alive in its own shell.

Thairyn's eyes blurred with tears. He hated Tindus. He hated this island. Why didn't his father come for him? He wanted to go home. Now his only real dream was gone. He stared at the rock in the fire. It was glowing red-orange. It looked more like the dragon egg—red, shiny, like liquid swirling over its surface. It must be just the tears in his eyes.

Suddenly, the rock wobbled. Thairyn gasped, sat up, and dragged his dirty sleeve across his eyes. Had the rock really moved? He glanced nervously at his sleeping captors, and then his eyes returned to the egg. It wobbled again. Thairyn's dying ember of hope suddenly rekindled.

Easing out of his bedroll, Thairyn inched toward the fire pit. The night air was cold and damp. He shivered. Did he dare hope for the impossible? What great magic was this?

The rock wobbled again. Then it rolled over. It rolled over and over until it was out of the fire pit completely and on the cold, sandy floor of the cave. It rolled right up to Thairyn. It looked just like it had at the Rhynstar Inn. It was beautiful, and Thairyn's heart leaped.

How had the egg changed itself? He had seen it looking like nothing more than a rough, gray rock. Now here it was, again looking like a polished blood-ruby as big as his hand! He reached down to pick it up but stopped, remembering it had just been in the fire for several hours. He would have to scuttle back for his blanket. Anxiously, he chanced a finger's quick touch on the egg.

Thairyn gasped and jerked his hand away. The egg was barely warm, and certainly cool enough to handle. How could that be? He plucked it up and scampered back to bed. He cradled it tenderly in his hands. He was so excited that he tingled all over.

Wait. He stilled himself. He did have a tingly feeling, but it was coming from the egg. All at once, the egg expanded, growing so large Thairyn could no longer conceal the egg in his hands. He turned his body away trying to shield the egg from view, though the men slept on.

"What am I going to do?" he asked himself. "How can I keep this hidden now?" He looked at the red, swirling colors. "What am I to do with you?" he whispered to the egg.

There was a slight niggle in the back of Thairyn's mind. He couldn't figure out what it meant. He listened, and felt it rather than heard it. There it was again! Then on the third time, it became clear. He knew what he should do. He could see in his mind another cave where he could hide the dragon's egg. It was perfect, and it would be safe. "I must go there now," Thairyn whispered to himself. "The morning will be too late."

Guards find Emija

CHAPTER 21

Thairyn ran through the wet brush and rocks in the dark. It was as if he had been there before, though he knew he never had. Yet somehow, he saw the way in his mind so clearly. His shoes and brown, linen pant-legs were soaked. He had no coat, but his soiled, white tunic offered some protection from the chill. His breath made small clouds in the cold air. Holding his precious egg tightly, he was glad the rain had stopped, and both moons were full, lighting the way.

Along the cliff's edge Thairyn ran. The cliff was dotted with caves of all sizes. Thairyn remembered his grandmother telling him the stories. All the caves were called "The Eyes on the Heart" because they looked out toward Heart Island. Sailors said the caves looked like a thousand eyes, and every now and then, one would show a flickering wink at night. He thought about their cave, wondering if their fire would show a wink in the night.

Suddenly, Thairyn stumbled, sending a shower of loose rock plummeting over the cliff. He fell, gasping, trying to keep himself from following the rocks over the edge. He glanced down at the crashing waves a hundred feet below. Shivering, he crawled away from the edge and continued on more carefully.

Then all at once, the moons went behind the clouds, and the night became very dark. Thairyn froze, unable to take a step safely. He thought of the fossi-shell in his pocket, but feared to show any light in case the men woke and found him gone. Several painful minutes passed as the boy crouched in the cold, wet blackness. When the moons finally cleared the clouds, Thairyn quickened his pace, worried was he running out of time.

At last, Thairyn came to the place he had seen in his mind. It was so familiar. Partially blocking the entrance of this cave was a mound of rocks. The rocks must have once been part of the cave wall. Stepping up onto the mound of rocks, Thairyn could see the black mouth of the cave gaping open, waiting for him. Taking a quick look around, the boy climbed down the mound and into the cave. It was pitch black inside, but dry.

"Good thing I brought a fossi-shell," Thairyn said to the egg he had cradled in is arm. He pulled the fossi-shell out and began to explore the cave. The cave was small, but not as small as the leavings cave. The floor was mostly pebbles. Thairyn tried squeezing into a fissure in the back wall. It was too narrow, even for him. The boy wandered a bit until he found a small sandy area around a bend of the uneven walls. This was the perfect spot. Thairyn dug a small hole. He gently laid the egg in the sand. It would be out of direct sight should anyone else enter the cave. He hated leaving the egg, but knew he must.

"Goodbye for now," he whispered. "I'll be back as soon as I can."

Back at the camping cave, Thairyn laid his wet shoes and pants near the fire pit and poked up the fire as he had seen the men do. There were only embers, but it still gave off a bit of warmth. He gently laid two small branches on the coals and hoped his things would dry before he had to put them on again. Thairyn was back in his bedroll sleeping before either of his captors awakened.

* * *

In the capital city of en'Edlia, it was the Grand Installation Day of the Ascending Oracle. At daybreak, a summons was to be delivered to the apprentice, requesting her appearance at the palace for this great honor and bestowal of title.

The honor guard consisted of three very fresh, very new recruits. This was their first assignment of importance, and at least one on them was very nervous. Their crisp, spotless uniforms of white, accented with green trim, nearly glowed in the faint light of pre-dawn.

"Wait till the sun hits these gold buttons!" remarked the tallest one of the three, his white-capped head held high. "I'm taking bets on whose will be brightest."

"Quiet, Roun! Don't get cocky. We got a job to do," seethed the redhead, named Jye, and the obvious leader of the group.

"Quiet in the ranks!" hissed Esga, straightening her own cap. She smiled as the other two snapped to and continued to march on.

The three moved through the streets without further conversation. No citizens turned out for this part of the occasion. The streets were quiet and deserted except for the light-stepping footfalls of the honor guard.

They soon reached the modest lodgings of the oracle's apprentice. With much ceremony, they knocked three times on the curved-top door and then came to attention to wait for an answer. They stood, anxious to salute smartly when the door opened. Several minutes passed in the quiet of the morning. A skitter sniffed around Roun's boots. He kicked it away as a seabird wheeled overhead, emitting a mournful cry.

"Shouldn't someone be answering the door by now?" whispered Roun.

"Quiet!" whispered Jye.

"I'm knocking again," said Esga.

"Wait!" squeaked out Jye, but it was too late. Another three knocks sounded loudly.

They leaned toward the door, hoping to hear sounds of someone scurrying to answer. The silence was eerie.

"What do we do now, Jye?" asked Roun.

"Our orders were to deliver this summons, which is what we are going to do."

"Well, we can't just leave it and run," remarked Esga. "It has to be hand delivered to the apprentice."

"Perhaps we should try the door," suggested Roun, reaching for the latch.

"Are you a crazy breakfast bug?" hissed Jye. "We are delivering a summons, not breaking and entering!"

"I'm not breaking anything," said Roun, shrugging.

Meanwhile, Esga grabbed the latch, and the door opened easily at her slight pressure.

"Gentlemen," she said to her companions. "I think we have a problem."

Roun and Jye stared through the open doorway along with Esga. Not three feet from them was the body of a young woman sprawled face down on the floor. She was dressed in the simple brown tunic of an apprentice.

After a few paralyzed seconds, Jye's training surfaced, and he took action. "Esga, contact the palace, get the healers here now. Roun, check the area for other victims or intruders— Go!"

Roun moved cautiously into the house, he had no weapon, except a short sword, but he needed none. Roun's birth-gift was bending things. Metal, wood, bones, whatever was needed.

Esga closed her eyes and sent her telepathic message. "They should be here just about . . ." she waited, ticking off the seconds. "Now!"

The healing team arrived through teleportation and immediately went to work.

"She's not dead, you know." Esga jumped at Roun's voice in her ear. She slugged his arm.

"How do you know?" Esga threw back.

"Saw her fingers move when I went by," Roun replied as he rubbed his arm. "That hurt!"

"Report!" Jye commanded as he stepped back outside the house.

"All's clear. No sign of intruders, inside or out. Nothing in the house has been disturbed that I can tell," Roun told him.

"Good. The healers are taking the apprentice to the palace immediately. Let's hope they do their job well. We need to report to the high patriarch on our assignment. Let's march!"

The three young guards took up their march double-time back to the palace.

Thairyn finds
the shards

Dan Whybark 2015

CHAPTER 22

The three stranded on Claw Island established a routine. Each morning, the men foraged for wood to keep the fire going and the damp chill from invading their cave. Thairyn helped them in order to keep Tindus from complaining. Once there was enough wood gathered for that day and into the next, the men would go to the stream to fish, lay snares, and gather edible plants and berries. Fortunately, the island had many resources. However, the limited quantities would not sustain them for long. Their purchased provisions were nearly exhausted, and it seemed unlikely that Naron would bring any more.

At first, Tindus had demanded the boy stay within sight as they foraged, but Arth finally convinced him that on an island, there was nowhere for the boy to go. Thairyn learned how to forage for himself too, eating safe berries and leaves as he went. Most days, while the men fished and argued between themselves, Thairyn scampered away to visit the egg.

Each day Thairyn found the egg larger than the day before. It was always warm to the touch now. He sat on the bumpy cave floor, cradling the egg in his lap, while he told it about his family and his life. He told it stories about his mother's world where no one had magic. He revealed his deepest wishes for a birth-gift, and that he was the best catch-me-if-you-can player. The glistening, ruby egg listened patiently to all Thairyn's words, feeling all his emotions.

From time to time, Thairyn thought the egg talked to him. He would feel little thoughts pop into his mind. He would smile and pretend the egg really was talking just to him. It made him feel less alone. He loved the egg and wanted to stay with it always. Eventually though, Arth would be calling after him, and he would have to go. The boy didn't want anyone, even Arth, knowing about the egg.

On the third day after hiding the egg, Thairyn came for his daily visit. As usual, he carefully slipped away, circled around, and then backtracked to reach the hiding cave. He could feel himself getting happier at the thought of having his hands on his precious dragon egg. He looked around cautiously before he entered the small cave. Then, he went straight to the sandy spot.

Sudden panic made the boy's heart leap. The egg was gone! Thairyn frantically scratched in the sand and hurriedly searched around in the cave. Where was his egg? Had one of the men found it? He was just ready to run back to their camping cave when his spied something among the rocks at the opening of the cave.

Bending over, Thairyn picked it up and cupped it in his hand. It was red, but not bright red. It was dull. A lifeless, red piece of something. It was thin, slightly curved, and had sharp, broken edges. Thairyn poked at it with his finger. What was it?

A whispering sound made Thairyn look up. He squinted, scanning the area. Suddenly, he saw more dull-red shards scattered among the rocks. It was almost like a trail.

Thairyn moved to follow the fragments. He didn't have to look far. Behind a large stone was the dragon egg, or what was left of it. The remaining pieces lay scattered in a small puddle of smelly goo. Thairyn had become so attached to the egg, he had forgotten that it just might hatch. He plucked up a large shell fragment and looked about sadly.

Then, a new feeling of panic made his heart feel like a heavy stone in his chest. The egg had been easy to hide, easy to care for. Now it had hatched! Now he had a baby dragon to hide and care for. This was not going to be so easy. "Where are you?" he whispered. "Are you all right?"

Thairyn continued his search, peering into bushes and around rocks. He was afraid to call out, so he whispered again, "Where are you?"

I'm here, a voice said clearly in his mind. Then a scene came vividly to his thoughts. He knew exactly where the hatchling was.

Reaching the spot quickly, he found the hatchling crouching among the rocks, munching on a large, brown-striped bug it had captured. The hatchling looked up, and popped the remains into its mouth as Thairyn approached. *I'm glad you have come,* said the voice in Thairyn's mind. *I don't like being alone.*

Thairyn looked deeply into the bright, golden eyes of the baby dragon, no higher than his knee. It blinked slowly at him, its eyes alive with intelligence.

"It was you who talked to me, even in the egg, wasn't it?" Thairyn spoke quietly, and he knelt by the hatchling.

Of course it was me. I can hear your thoughts and your words, and you can hear mine. I am Strepenkluus."

"Strep . . . what?"

Stre—pen—kluus, the hatchling repeated more slowly.

"Can I just call you . . . um . . . um . . . Kluus?" Thairyn asked.

Kluus? Kluus. Yes. I like it.

"So, Kluus, what do I do now? Do I have to be your mother?"

Oh, no, I am not like humans. I do not need a mother.

"Will you leave me then, Kluus?" Thairyn said sadly, already feeling lonely at the thought.

Kluus jumped and squeaked, *Thairyn—*

"You know my name?"

Yes, I know many things about you. Everything you told the egg, you told to me. Thairyn and Kluus are bonded now. I will be with you always.

"Bonded? What does that mean?" Thairyn asked anxiously.

It means that I am part of you, and you are part of me. It will cause us pain to be apart. We will feel greater joy when we are together. One will not be whole without the other. We will be together always. Do you understand?

Thairyn smiled broadly, then could not contain his joy and laughed aloud. He reached out to the dragon, which hopped into his lap and rubbed its head on his chest. Thairyn inspected his new companion more closely. Kluus was a bright ruby color with a darker underbelly. Its skin was scaly, yet felt sleek and smooth as he stroked it. Small knobs ran down its back. Kluus explained that those would be its back ridge. Its tiny, deep-purple wings quivered when Thairyn used his finger to scratch under Kluus's chin. A contented thrumming came from its throat. Thairyn was elated!

"Jonx! Boy! Where are ye?"

Thairyn froze at the sound of Arth's call. The man wasn't close, but coming. *Now what do I do?* His thoughts whirled around in circles. In his panic, he plucked up the hatchling and ran for the hiding cave.

Why are you so afraid? I can take care of myself. The small dragon projected into the boy's mind.

"I don't want them to find and catch you. They will hurt or kill you. I just know it! I must protect you."

It is I who will soon protect you. I will grow quickly now that I am out of the confines of my shell. Leave me in the cave. They will never catch me. I must forage for food. I need fuel to grow.

"But I don't want to leave you. I'm afraid I will lose you," Thairyn looked pitifully at the hatchling. It was a baby, yet seemingly wiser than he was.

I can always be in your thoughts now, even when we are apart. Speak with your mind, and I will hear.

"All right," Thairyn said sadly, turning to go. He stopped at the mouth of the cave, looking back at Kluus. "Promise you won't leave me?"

Kluus looked up at Thairyn, its golden eyes shining. *I couldn't even if I wanted to. We are bonded, you and I, forever. I am your dragon. You are my rider.*

"Me?" Thairyn gasped. "I'm going to be a dragon rider?"

Yes. You have the gift of dragon speech. You quickened my egg. Only a true rider can do that.

"Great slimy sea slugs! I have a birth-gift after all!" he gasped. "Wait till my sisters find out! And Father!" Thairyn smiled and jumped into the air. "When will I get a ride? You are so small now."

Soon, Thairyn. Go quickly now. The other human is coming. Arth, is it?

"Yes. I'll go," said Thairyn, and he clambered away over the rocks.

Emija awakens

CHAPTER 23

E mija opened her eyes. Disoriented, she looked around the unfamiliar room. She glimpsed the back of a stranger bent over a basin washing her hands. *Perhaps I have died and this is the great beyond,* thought the apprentice as she noticed the fine furnishings of the room. The heavy, deep-green velvet draperies veiled most of the window's light. The pale pink bedding was exquisitely soft and silky. Intricate shell-shaped vases in all sizes were scattered around the room. Some of the vases held fragrant flowers in a variety of vibrant colors. Everything in the room spoke of wealth and richness. *If this is the great beyond,* she thought, *I like it!*

She took inventory of her own body. No serious pains. She wiggled her toes and fingers. Everything seems to be working, but a little stiff and achy. She tried sitting up. The room began to spin, and there was a dull pounding in her head. "Oh," she sighed, lying back again.

Instantly, the activity in the room increased. The stranger hurried to her side and then called to someone else, who ran out of the room. The dark face of the stranger came close, her black curly hair hanging down to her shoulders. She looked deeply into Emija's eyes, but the apprentice was having trouble focusing.

"Emija, can you hear me?" the stranger said to her gently.

The spinning was slowing to a stop, while the pounding was ebbing away. The apprentice looked up into the kind, dark eyes of the stranger. "Who are you?" she asked. "Where am I?"

"I am Neepha, a healer. You are in a palace healing room. Do you know who you are?"

Emija thought that was a dumb question. "Of course I know who I am! I'm the oracle's apprentice, Emija. I have important information for the high patriarch about—"

"Well, not right now," replied Neepha, straightening her crisp white apron. "You have been very ill and need to finish recovering."

Trying to push herself up again, Emija cried, "You have to send for the high patriarch! I must tell him—"

"Calm yourself, apprentice." Neepha gently pushed Emija back down into a lying position. "I have already called for the high patriarch."

Hearing this, Emija lay back and relaxed. Neepha smiled and brought her some water.

"How long have I been here?"

"Since you were found unconscious in your home two days ago."

"Two days ago!" Emija exclaimed. "What happened?"

"That's what we have been trying to figure out. Do you remember anything?"

The apprentice searched her memory. *What had happened?*

Just then, High Patriarch Merrick burst into the room. "Thank the healers you're all right!" he cried, and came to sit by her bedside. "How are you feeling?"

"Never mind me," Emija declared. "I found out some information about Thairyn."

"Thairyn? But how?"

The memory of what she had done came flooding back to her mind. She told Merrick everything. "So he was at Dragon's Landing and, wherever they went next, which was probably south and east, your son has a dragon's egg with him," the apprentice finished.

"Amazing!" cried Merrick. "Your gifts are impressive."

The apprentice looked down, her checks reddening at the compliment. "I'm sorry I'm late for the installation," Emija continued meekly.

"Never mind," Merrick said quietly. "We have postponed it until you are ready. You tell me when."

"Thank you, High Patriarch. I guess I over-extended my abilities too much at once. It was your daughters who asked me to help in the search."

"The twins? But I specifically told everyone—"

"They asked me to help as their friend, not as oracle. How could I refuse the plea of my sweet friends?"

Merrick shook his head. "Those girls!"

"Don't be angry with them. They love their brother and feel helpless to do anything. They feel very left out."

Merrick sat quietly for a moment. "I guess I have been so focused on finding my son that I've forgotten about my daughters." He lowered his head in thought. "I am grateful you were willing to risk it. Your information will help. Our trail had grown cold, but now we can renew our efforts in the right direction with the added description of another kidnapper. Thank you, Emija."

Neepha came forward and said, "Your Highness, the apprentice needs to rest now."

Merrick looked up at the healer. "You know best, Neepha. Get her up and moving soon. I need an oracle as soon as possible." He stood and smiled at Emija. "Krystin and the twins will be by to visit when you're up to it. I know Ardloh would be very proud of you," he said warmly, and then he turned and left the room.

Naron
threatens
Thauryn

CHAPTER 24

A week after the hatching, late in the morning, Naron arrived on Claw Island like a hurricane. He was in a foul mood and raging like the east winds. The ransom had not been delivered, and he was furious.

"They think I don't mean business! Do they think I won't kill the little crown? Well, I'll show them! They will pay me or watch their son pay dearly, just as I paid for me parent's carelessness!" Naron shouted and swore at everyone and no one. He stomped about, pacing back and forth, in and out of the cave.

"So what now?" he roared at the other men.

"Well, ye could—" ventured Tindus.

"Silence, bumphead! Who asked ye?" Naron yelled, pausing only a moment in his pacing.

Naron's anger held the others prisoner in the cave. They dare not speak or move. Tindus tried to edge out of the cave, but Naron dragged him back and accused him of deserting.

"I have to go a step further now," seethed Naron. "I know what I'll do! I'll cut off the boy's finger and send it to thems in the palace. Or maybe his whole hand!" He glared at Thairyn, while drawing his knife, which gleamed red in the firelight.

"No, Naron," Arth's voice was low. "I'll not let ye hurt the boy."

"Try and stop me! What does it matter? No one worried about hurting me when I was a boy. It's ye who's going to kill him anyway."

"Arth?" Thairyn croaked out. "You . . . you're going to k . . . k . . . kill me?"

Arth angrily looked at Naron, then pleadingly at the boy. "No, I wouldn't. I couldn't, boy.

"Ye're a traitor then," yelled Naron. "If ye don't kill the boy, like I said, then I will, and ye'll watch."

"Ye'll have to kill me first." Arth stepped forward. "I won't let ye harm the boy."

Thairyn scuttled away from Naron until his back hit the rocks. He crawled to a standing position, getting ready to dodge his attacker and run for the cave entrance. *Kluus, help me!* he thought desperately.

I'm coming! Kluus's thoughts entered the boy's mind.

Naron continued to advance toward Thairyn. "Wait!" Tindus grabbed Naron's arm. "Let me do it," he smiled wickedly. "It will do me good to pay back some of the pain that brat's been to me."

Naron's eyes were cold and deadly. His gaze slowly moved from Tindus's face to the man's hand on his arm. Tindus paled. He withdrew his hand and took a step back. "Beggin' yer pardon, Naron. Do . . . do as ye wish, of course," he sputtered.

Naron turned to look at the wide-eyed boy, and then back at the now-timid Tindus. He glanced at Arth who stood rigidly determined with his fists clenched. For a moment, there was no sound but the crackling fire and the breathing of the cave's occupants. Naron smiled, and then suddenly laughed loudly.

"What a bunch of breakfast bugs ye are!" Naron burst out. "Do ye think I want to hear the brat screamin' and cryin' the whole time I'm here? Do ye think I want to carry back a rotting, stinking piece of the little crown? Oh, no! We'll wait till tomorrow. Then, I'll send the new message off to his dear patria, nice and fresh." Naron continued to laugh as he put his knife away. "When do we eat?"

For an instant, the light from outside the cave was blocked. There was a sound like a ship's sails snapping in a strong wind.

"What was that?" Naron asked in amazement.

"We thinks it might be a large bird of some kind," Tindus burst out. "Never seen it close up, only far off. Might be fishing off the island."

"I want to see this," Naron replied, and strode out of the cave closely followed by the others.

They gazed up into the sky, shading their eyes against the midday sun. "There!" shouted Tindus. "Just going over the cliffs toward the sea."

Everyone turned to look. All they saw was a flash of red disappear down out of sight. They stood watching, waiting for the thing to reappear.

"Maybe we can bring it down and have sea-chicken instead of more fish," Naron said.

Thairyn began inching away from the men. When he was about ten feet away from Arth, he broke out into a run. The sudden noise and motion caught his captors' attention. The men all turned at once to see the boy tearing off in the opposite direction.

"Well! Get him, ye bottom spiders! Get him!" Naron barked.

Tindus took off at a gallop, but Arth walked slowly away.

"Ye're wearing on me nerves, Arth," Naron called after him. "Best hope this ends quickly now, and we can part company while ye're still living."

Ignoring Naron, Arth continued to plod along. He called over his shoulder, "Best see to yer boat, Naron, lest the boy make off with it. Yer threats have got him scared real bad. He's liable to do anything."

Cursing, Naron loped off toward Talon Beach, where he had dragged the boat up onto shore. "If he steals the boat, I'll kill him right there. Then I'll still cut off his finger for the ransom!"

CHAPTER 25

Thairyn ran.

Kluus! They are going to kill me! Or cut me up or something. What should I do? Where can I hide?

Stop running so I can come to get you.

Come to get me? What do you mean?

You'll see. Here I come!

Thairyn stopped and looked up. He scanned the horizon. All at once, a great gust of wind at his back knocked him to the ground. He heard Kluus's chuckling sound, which was more like a rumbling in its throat.

Sorry. That was a little too hard. I'm still learning.

Thairyn rolled over to see Kluus. He looked where he thought Kluus should be. He saw only legs—big, red, scaly dragon legs. Thairyn threw his head back to see the whole dragon, nearly cracking his head on the ground. Kluus was huge! It had quadrupled in size and now towered above him. Its wings, stretched out longer than Naron's boat, were bright red as the sun lit them from behind. Kluus's chest was bigger than a wharf barrel. Its scaled legs and forearms rippled with muscles. The spikes on its back ridge were as long as Thairyn's arm. Its tail trailed out behind it like a huge, ridged snake, twitching with energy.

"You got big!" Thairyn cried.

Kluus's laugh rumbled in its throat. *I guess you could say so. It has been three days since you saw me last. I was getting lonely.*

I'm sorry, Kluus. But there was lots of rain and then Naron—

Never mind, Thairyn. Want a ride?

"Sure!" Thairyn shouted aloud.

What about him? Kluus asked.

Thairyn turned to see Tindus frozen in his tracks, staring at Kluus.

"Oh, him? Maybe you could scare him away. He's mean."

Kluus turned toward Tindus and rising up, spread his wings wide. Tindus began to take a step backwards. Kluus let out a tremendous roar, and shook its head fiercely, showing its very sharp, pointed teeth. Tindus stumbled and fell down.

Can I singe him a bit? Kluus chortled.

Thairyn's mouth popped open. "You can breathe fire? Great slimy sea slugs!"

Tindus scrambled to his feet and then dashed away, screaming loudly for help.

"I don't think you need to." Thairyn replied and then smiled broadly. "I'll be just fine with you around." Thairyn threw his arms around the red beast's leg and pressed his cheek against its warm, scaly surface.

Kluus mentally showed Thairyn how to climb up its front leg, grab a spike on its back ridge, and take a seat in front of its wing joints.

Are you settled?

"I think so."

Then hold on tight! Up we go! Kluus flapped once, twice, and they lifted off the ground.

"Woohoo!" Thairyn yelled as they soared over the running-scared Tindus. "No one will ever catch me again!" The boy's blond hair whipped back from his dirty face as he clung to the ridge spike. His clothes fluttered and snapped around him. Suddenly, he felt himself losing his seat as Kluus increased speed and changed direction. "Kluus! I'm slipping!"

Squeeze my neck with your knees and lean in close to the spike. Pull yourself close to me. Be one with me, Thairyn.

Thairyn struggled to adjust his position without losing his grip. He snugged in his knees and hugged the spike with all his might. Feeling more secure, he stilled his body then, concentrating on being one with the dragon. No, not *the* dragon— HIS DRAGON!

With his heart leaping in his chest, Thairyn began to sense Kluus's movements. He felt the tilt and angle of its wings as Kluus adjusted with the winds. He felt his body shift and lean to follow Kluus's every move. He even began to feel as if he were flying, not just riding. His spirit soared higher than his body. He felt such joy, his tears made wet trails into his ears.

Now you are becoming a rider! The dragon's voice came softly to his thoughts.

"Oh, Kluus! Teach me everything. I want to be the best rider on Irth!"

And so you shall!

They soared for several more minutes, banking and diving over the men as they ducked and ran. Thairyn laughed and whooped as he grew more confident on Kluus's back.

Glancing down again, Thairyn saw something that instantly stopped his joy. His heart turned cold. "Kluus! We must help Arth!"

*   *   *

As soon as Naron had seen Thairyn on the dragon, he came back looking for the other men. He found Tindus sweating and pale, babbling about the dragon. Arth had been harder to find. When he did, Naron attacked Arth, punching, kicking, cursing and screaming.

Arth was a big man. He defended himself by blocking Naron's blows and dodging the kicks. Naron then drew his knife, slashing out at Arth, who backed away, putting some distance between himself the edge of Naron's blade.

".Ye have ruined all me work and plans!" Naron growled. "How could ye let this happen? I'll kill ye for this!" His fury drove him on.

Naron kept stalking Arth with deadly intent, his face nearly purple with rage. Arth began picking up rocks, looking for any means of defense.

"Stay back, Naron. I don't want to hurt ye. I never wanted to hurt anyone."

Naron cursed. "Ye're born a ruglump, and now ye'll die one."

Naron easily dodged the few rocks that Arth halfheartedly tossed toward him. "Naron, stop! Please!" Arth cried out. "Let the boy go. There's nothing ye can do now."

"No! I'll not stop! This was for me parents, who died for no reason! This was for me grandfather, banished from Irth, then killed by that she-witch of a matriarch. This was for the child I never got to be, the life I never had. This was for everything! All the hurt, all the tears, all the grief and loss. I'll not stop now! Not for ye, or anyone else! I will have me revenge!"

Naron darted forth, lunging at Arth. The big man caught his attacker's wrists, holding him off as they struggled together. Arth and Naron were locked hand-to-hand, while Naron tried to force his blade ever closer to his opponent's chest.

Kluus went into a dive right at the fighting men. The boy and his dragon plunged straight down, the wind howling around them.

Suddenly, the dragon's wings spread wide. Its clawed feet splayed out, intent on the capture of its prey. Tindus cried out at the approach of the great, red beast.

The strugglers looked up just as Kluus closed its claws around Arth's shoulders and lifted both men off the ground. Instantly, Arth shouted out in shock and fear, and then released Naron, who fell back to the ground with a thud.

With a mighty flap of its blood-red wings, Kluus gained altitude. Naron leapt to his feet and threw his knife at Arth with all his might. Naron's blade whistled through the air, finding its mark in Arth's leg. The big man cried out in pain, but could do nothing hanging in the dragon's grasp. Naron threw rocks at the dragon, but all fell short. He cursed and stomped as his prize, along with his chance for revenge, flew away.

Naron's anger was not played out in the least. Seeing Tindus cowering on the ground, while the dragon carried off its passengers, brought out the last of his fury. Tindus leapt up and ran as if he were being chased by a demon, which wasn't far from the truth. Naron gave chase, cursing while pelting him with stones. Each man tried to gain ground on the other.

* * *

Thairyn had to smile at the sight of two tiny men running across the island. They looked like ants. "Will Arth be all right, Kluus?" he asked, glancing down at the terror-stricken man dangling from the dragon's claws.

He is perfectly safe, Kluus replied.

"Well he doesn't look like he's enjoying the ride as much as I am. Can you carry him on your back along with me?"

Very well, but it will be a bit squishy for you.

"That's all right. I'm used to being close to Arth," Thairyn replied as he patted Kluus on the neck. He leaned over and yelled down to Arth, "Don't worry, Arth! We will land, and then you can ride up here with me."

Looking up anxiously, Arth managed a teeth-gritting grimace.

Upon landing, Thairyn realized Arth was wounded. Not only had Naron's knife given the big man a deep cut, but Kluus's claws had scraped Arth's skin causing painful welts on his sides and arms. Thairyn fussed and cried, but the big man just ripped off a piece of his own shirt and bound up his leg. There was nothing to be done about the welts. "I'm not going to die from them," Arth told the boy. Still, Thairyn was anxious to get Arth to the palace healers.

Minutes later, now with two atop, Kluus was aloft again, sailing on the east wind due northwest toward Dragon's Landing and Thairyn's home beyond.

Alarm-cock

Nan Whybark 2015

CHAPTER 26

T indus ran for his very life. He was sweating not just from exertion, but also from fear. Powered by adrenaline, he was fleet of foot and quickly put more distance between Naron and himself.

Tindus ran on through the low brush and rocky terrain without even glancing behind him. As Dragon Tooth peak came into view, he slowed to a winded, side-aching lope. Finally, he took the time to glance behind him. Naron was nowhere in sight. He was tempted to stop and catch his breath, but he knew Naron would be relentless. He pushed himself on, alternating between a fast walk and a gentle run.

The small man berated himself for getting involved with Naron in the first place. What had he been thinking? He knew Naron's reputation, but hoped to make a good sum of pa'trees in a short time. This deal had turned sour, and now deadly. For all his work and effort, suffering and pain, he would be lucky to escape with his life. It was just his fate, it would seem.

Tindus began to feel there might be hope of escape or concealment until Naron calmed down. He stopped quickly to slurp up some water at a creek. Maybe they'd go east now and spend some time in the City of the Lost. Make themselves scarce for a while, then Naron would have time to . . . *Hold onto yer breeches, Tindus me boy!* he thought to himself.

A new thought occurred to Tindus. "If I take the boat, Naron will be stranded on Claw Island. Maybe for a long, long time." Tindus's sweating face broke into a wide grin. "Maybe forever." He laughed wickedly, increasing his pace. "Maybe I could turn *him* in for a reward, or at least in exchange for the information on his whereabouts." This was getting better and better.

* * *

Naron stood next to Serpent's Tongue Creek, bent in half, gasping for breath. He was younger than Tindus, but the struggle with Arth had wearied him. The scrawny bumphead had outdistanced him for now. He could not let him leave the island. Better yet, *he* would leave the island without that irritating bottom-spider.

Grunting as he straightened up, Naron ran on. He had to catch up with Tindus, and he knew a shortcut to the beach.

* * *

Tindus reached the beach and spotted the boat. He was exhausted, but fear pushed him on. He pulled and tugged the heavy craft through the deep sand. Slowly it moved, inch by inch towards the water's edge. His breathing was harsh, and his muscles screamed with every movement. Finally, he felt the water lift the boat to floating. He slogged out through the salty surf, pushing the boat, and then he hefted himself into the craft and sprawled over the seat.

Suddenly, he heard Naron's voice cursing and yelling. Tindus peered over the edge of the boat. Naron was in the water, moving quickly within reach of the boat. Tindus fumbled for the oars, barely getting them into the water. Naron lunged for the edge of the craft, missed, recovered, and lunged again. His fingers caught the edge, pulling the end of the boat down. He splashed wildly as he tried to haul himself up.

Grabbing one oar with both hands, Tindus swung it around and brought it down forcefully on Naron's fingers. Naron howled in pain and anger. "I'll kill ye!" he screamed.

Again, Tindus clubbed Naron's already blue fingers with the oar. Naron cried out and released the edge, floundering in the deeper water. The little man recovered and pulled hard on the oars, rowing away. Naron tried to regain his stroke, swimming for the boat again.

Tindus steadily pulled away from his pursuer until Naron was just a small bump on the water's surface. *Catch me if you can!* he thought. He slowed then to give his aching muscles and panting breath a chance to recover. He didn't dare stop, though. He was damp with sweat. If he got cold, his muscles would cramp up, and he'd be done for. He must make the shore and then get far away. He smiled to himself. A nice quiet inn would be just the place where he could send off a quick catlin to the high patriarch on just where to find the kidnapper of his son. That is, if the information was worth a small sum to his highness. *Yes,* he thought, *this might turn out well after all.* He laughed aloud when he saw Naron drag himself back onto the beach, where he yelled dreaded oaths of revenge and threats of death at Tindus long after the boat-thief ceased to hear him.

In Tindus's condition and alone, the crossing to the mainland took an agonizingly long time. Just after dark, he finally tied the craft up to the dock and then collapsed in an exhausted heap along the grassy trail that led to the boat master's hut.

In the early hours of the next morning, Tindus woke feeling sore and weak. A shadow fell across him. He rolled onto his back, squinted his eyes, and tried to focus.

"Brought back the boat, have ye?" said the boat master, standing over him with his long, unkempt beard nearly dragging on the ground.

Tindus could only nod and struggle wearily to his feet.

"That be good, but where are yer traveling companions?" asked the boat master.

Shrugging, Tindus turned away from the old man's glare, looking for the path to the road. He had forgotten about the boat master. He didn't want to talk to this ancient lunatic, much less look into those purple eyes of his. He just wanted to be on his way. He was free now. Free from Naron's anger and personal plan of revenge. He was free from babysitting that royal brat. He was tired of the whole thing. He just wanted to find a quiet place to rest and move on with his new plan. He would have to be careful, to be sure. Naron wouldn't remain stranded on the island forever. There should be enough time to make himself disappear for a long time, and perhaps live comfortably, if all went as he planned.

"And what of me prophecy?" the boat master asked, interrupting Tindus's thoughts. "Has it come to pass? Of course ye remember it."

Tindus had no idea what he was talking about. "What prophecy?" he asked, though not interested.

The old man didn't speak, yet the words echoed in Tindus's mind.

"One will never return this way. One will die. And one will be changed forever."

Tindus smiled to himself. That had nothing to do with him. For all he knew Arth was already dead in the claws of that accursed dragon. Served him right. The boy obviously wasn't coming back this way. Little brats should never be trusted. Naron was changed all right—no longer the fearless leader. Tindus almost laughed aloud at the thought.

All at once, gnarled fingers gripped Tindus's shoulder, spinning him around. Abruptly, he was staring into the eyes of the boat master. He felt fear creep up his legs, wriggle through his belly, and place its clammy hands around his heart. He was caught and held spellbound by those purple, red-rimmed eyes, Tindus had no power within himself to break free. Again, the ancient one spoke in a quiet voice, which did nothing to ease Tindus's fear.

"I see ye are a fearful, greedy, little man. Ye have no thoughts except for yerself. That is sad; very sad." The boat master shook his head and sighed. "Do ye see those animals in my yard?"

Tindus tried to look, but could not. Yet, he could see in his mind exactly what the master wanted him to see.

"The ones with the skinny, yellow legs and ruffling, black feathers? Those poor little things scratch all day trying to find a speck of food. And I feed them. Yes, I feed them, and they all run to the food, pecking at each other in greed. They spend so much effort keeping all the others away that they don't eat what is in front of them. So the other animals come to snuffle it up, and those poor creatures are left to scratch at the dirt looking for what some might have lost."

In his mind, Tindus could see the creature's beady eyes and sharp beak. He watched the quick, jerking motions of its head, searching and watchful for any opportunity. It stalked about suspiciously pecking at others who came too near.

Why is he showing this to me? thought Tindus. *Let me go!* his mind cried out. *Let me go!*

"Oh, no," the old man whispered as if he could hear Tindus's thoughts. "I fear ye are much like these poor creatures, Tindus," the boat master continued in his maddeningly calm voice. "I fear ye are so much like them, ye have become one of them. Did I tell ye they are called alarm-cocks?"

What? Tindus thought wildly. *What is he saying? How does he know my name? What crazy talk is this?*

Then, Tindus felt a strange dizziness sweep over him. He felt like his head—no, his whole body—was whirling around, faster and faster. He still gazed at the ancient man before him who seemed to be growing taller and taller, towering over him. He finally was able to look down at himself. His legs, that looked unusually yellow and thin, stood in a pile of too-big clothes. Something at his neck was itching. He reached up to scratch at it. Feathers brushed his face. Tindus held out his hands, but there were no fingers of flesh, only feathery appendages.

Horror-struck, Tindus cried out, "What have ye done to me?" His mind heard the words, but his ears heard, "Baaaaarrrrrruuuuuuuuccccckkkk?"

The boat master again shook his head and sighed. "Poor miserable creature. Poor little alarm-cock! So fearful, so anxious, but I shall help ye."

Tindus felt huge hands lift him off the ground. He struggled and fluttered to get away, but he was caught and held fast.

"Come with me to the shed where yer fears and anxiety will cease. Ye will join me for dinner, of course." The boat master stroked Tindus gently. "There, there now. No need to worry. It will all be over soon."

Tindus began to relax. His mind was growing hazy. *What were his plans? Where was he going to go?* He couldn't seem to remember.

Then, they were in the shed. It felt cool and dark. Tindus relaxed even more. This is what he wanted—to hide and rest. To escape being caught by—who was it?

The boat master took down his hatchet from the shed wall, and with a practiced swing, took the head off the little alarm-cock in his hand. "I've been hungry for cock stew for quite a while now," he said, with a small smile. "And so the prophecy is fulfilled, and Irth has become a little less wicked."

Emija sees a vision

CHAPTER 27

Kluus, with its passengers, sailed over Dragon's Landing, then angled west across en'Edlia Bay straight toward the capital city of en'Edlia. Thairyn could not stop grinning. He had a birth-gift! He had a dragon! He was going to be—*no—I am a dragon rider!* He couldn't wait to see his sisters' faces. And his father! What would his father say? His mother would cry. She always cried over her children. *What if she doesn't like me flying around on a dragon?* Thairyn thought worriedly.

Then we'll convince her otherwise, Thairyn heard Kluus say in his mind.

Thairyn patted his dragon. *Bonded for life*, he thought. *I'm going to love this! I love you, Kluus!*

Suddenly, Thairyn felt a tremor behind him. He glanced back at Arth. "You all right?" the boy called over the sound of the wind. Arth gave a stiff nod, but the big man didn't look all right. His face was white, his eyes were jammed shut, and he was visibly trembling. "We'll be home soon!" hollered the boy. *Hurry, Kluus! Hurry!*

*　*　*

Arth could not stop shaking. He was afraid of heights, and to make matters worse, he was on a moving dragon. Arth gripped the back ridge spike with all his might. He felt weak and light-headed. His leg hurt from the knife wound. His sides burned from the welts caused by the dragon's claws plucking him up. He knew he was heading for a death sentence, or worse—life in prison for his part in the kidnapping. *I can't escape this time*, he thought to himself. He shook his head thinking of his wife and children. He would not get the chance to make things right with them.

The big man peered at the boy in front of him. Thairyn's whole life would really begin now. *Mine will end,* thought Arth. *Strange how some things turn out just the opposite of what was first planned. I caught the boy, now the boy has caught me.* He glanced down for a moment. Maybe he should just let go of the spike and fall to his death. However, he couldn't get his fingers to loosen their white-knuckled grip. He closed his eyes again, tears blurring his vision. He was doomed.

*　*　*

High Patriarch Merrick stood on the palace veranda arrayed in his finest. His crown, which he seldom wore, gleamed on his brow. Beside him were his wife, Crown Matriarch Krystin, his mother, High Matriarch Narrian, and his daughters, Phyre and Jewl. Also seated there, were Merrick's two younger brothers, Jarrius and Wayen, and his sister, Nizza. Even Prince David, Krystin's younger brother, had come. All were painfully aware of the absence of Crown Patriarch Thairyn for this grand occasion.

The palace guard were dazzling in their white dress uniforms. The emerald, flying-shell flags of en'Edlia lined the boulevard and fluttered gently. The crowded lawn and boulevard before the palace were filled with the citizens of the city and beyond. On the right, a few from po'Enay waited, their dark heads rising above the rest. Clustered in the front, their white hair like beacons in the sunlight, am'Orans chattered excitedly. Even the Great Altere himself, with representatives from the tribes of the Altere Mountains, were shuffling uneasily at the crowd's edge.

Suddenly, the trumpets sounded, their clear blast silencing the crowd. The high patriarch stepped forward and spread his arms wide in welcome.

"Citizens of en'Edlia! Friends! Revered people of Irth! I, High Patriarch Merrick of the realm of en'Edlia, welcome you to the Installation Ceremony of the Ascending Oracle. We have waited long for this day, though we still grieve the passing over of our esteemed Oracle Ardloh. Yet let us not dampen this day with tears of sorrow, but with tears of joy as we embrace our bright future under the guidance of our new oracle, duly apprenticed and trained under the watchful care of the great Ardloh. It gives me great pleasure to present Oracle Emija!"

A roar of applause and shouts of approval erupted from the crowd as Emija stepped from behind the royal party. She bowed deeply to the royal family before she moved to stand beside the high patriarch. No longer in the brown apprentice robes, her rich emerald robe, embroidered with gold runes, shone in the sunlight. She gripped her newly carved staff at her side. She was glad to have it to steady her quaking knees. *Perhaps this is why an oracle has a staff,* she though grimly.

Merrick held up his hands for quiet. "Today, and henceforth," he announced loudly. "I declare Emija le'Anga oracle of en'Edlia until her passing. She will serve as counsel to the high patriarchal family, and as a member of the high council, to advise, counsel, and act as she sees fit to aid and guide en'Edlia of Irth. I command all to give her the respect and honor she deserves as oracle, and all to follow her guidance as she sees fit to give it."

The high patriarch handed the new oracle the scroll given him by Ardloh, and placed around her neck a green ribbon on which hung a white-winged shell, the emblem of en'Edlia. He embraced her, and then presented her to the gathering.

Cheers and tears flowed freely among royalty and all alike. It was a glorious day of celebration—one not had in en'Edlia for more than two hundred years. None was alive who remembered the last. There would be feasting and celebrating for three days to come. Yet a trace of gloom hung over the city for the still missing Crown Patriarch Thairyn.

Emija stood before the quieting crowd, which expectantly waited for her first inspired words as oracle. She felt the weight of her calling bearing down on her. She clung to her staff to steady herself. What could she say now to give hope and reassurance to the people? What could she do now to bring back young Thairyn? Her mind fogged and then suddenly cleared. She would do whatever was necessary. A sudden strength coursed through her as she felt Ardloh's influence.

You are the oracle! Now act like one! his words echoed in her mind.

Emija gazed off into the distance, stretching her vision beyond normal sight. There was something there, moving swiftly toward her. She could feel a great excitement in that ruby object. Suddenly, a realization solidified in her mind. She raised her staff and spoke out.

"High Patriarch Merrick, gathered en'Edlians and friends of Irth! Thank you for your warm acceptance. As oracle, I pledge my life to your service." Emija paused, looking out again at the approaching object. Raising her staff higher, she proclaimed, "I have seen a vision!"

A hush fell over the gathering. Some gasps of expectation went sputtering through the crowd. When all was quiet, Emija continued in a loud voice.

"I have seen Crown Prince Thairyn. He is safe and well. He will be returning home this very day. However, he returns not as he left. He returns with power and magic! His birth-gift has been revealed!"

At this statement, Merrick's eyes went wide, and he turned to draw his wife close. Krystin's eyes filled with tears as she hugged her husband. The twins jumped from their seats to join their parents. They clung to the new hope given them by Emija's declaration. All eyes were upon the oracle now.

Standing with staff still raised, the oracle again raised her voice. "There! See! He comes, riding his ruby dragon! Crown Patriarch Thairyn returns!"

All heads turned in the direction indicated by the oracle. All eyes squinted and peered into the distance, anxious to see this great sight. A bright, red speck, lit by the lowering sun, grew larger as the seconds passed into minutes. A great shout went up as it become recognizable. The ruby dragon came on steadily, and then it began to descend. Hastily, people backed away and cleared a place on the lawn for it to land.

Kluus, fanning its wings back to slow its descent, touched down with its hind legs first, making a rumbling THUD. It lowered its upper body down carefully until it was standing on all fours. Folding back its huge wings, it kneeled to allow its passengers to safely dismount.

The oracle could see that Thairyn needed no encouragement. He raced across the lawn toward the palace veranda. His family met and embraced him on the boulevard as the amazed crowd clamored around Arth and the dragon.

* * *

Supposing Arth to be Thairyn's rescuer, the crowd's movement carried the big man forward to the patriarchal family, much to his embarrassment and protest. Unable to escape, Arth stood before the family whose only son he had taken. He watched their joyful reunion and tearful outpouring of love. How could he have done such a terrible thing? What had been his motive, but lust for money and the goading of a supposed friend? He hung his head in shame. The boat master had judged him rightly. He had failed his own family and left them without means of support to chase his own greed. Now faced with consequences for his misdeeds, he hoped for death to end his miserable existence.

Suddenly, there was a quieting of the crowd, and Arth felt a small hand take his own. He raised his eyes to see Thairyn looking up at him with a smile.

"Come on, Arth! My family wants to meet you."

Fear sprang up in the big man's chest as the boy pulled at him. He wanted to run and hide, not face the high patriarch. Then, there he was, Merrick, High Patriarch of en'Edlia, grasping his hand, pumping his arm, slapping him on the back. *What was he saying?*

". . . and Thairyn has told us how you helped him and protected him. He says he would be dead if it hadn't been for you!" Then leaning in closely to Arth's ear, Merrick whispered, "We will discuss this in greater detail later, Arth, but for now, consider this a pardon for your crimes. You will stay with us at the palace until this is sorted out."

Arth numbly nodded. *A pardon? Did he hear that right?* He allowed his heart a tiny bit of hope. Perhaps—just perhaps—he could return to his own family with some respect. Would they accept him after all that had happened?

* * *

The high patriarch announced the festivities of the day could begin, so the crowd dispersed to play games, eat, and be entertained. The patriarchal family moved away into the palace for some private time with Thairyn and the oracle. The palace guard took up posts on either side of Arth and escorted him into a holding cell, then healers would be called to attend to his wounds.

In the family chambers, Thairyn poured out his adventure, the family experiencing his terror and delight, his pain and joy. They were amazed at his birth-gift and awed by how it had been revealed. The twins laughed when Thairyn told how he had taken on the name of Jonx and called Arth his patria. He glanced nervously at the frown on his father's face, but continued when his mother smiled. He explained how Arth had helped him endure the harsh treatment of his other captors, and how he had protected him from Naron's knife at the risk of his own life.

"And I'm a dragon rider!" Thairyn burst out for the fifth time. There had not been one in the family for generations. It was a great addition to the power and influence of the patriarchal family line. There could be no doubt now. Thairyn would inherit the throne of en'Edlia. Even the Xens would not dare object, for Thairyn was Irth-born with a powerful birth-gift.

"I'm so proud of you, son!" Merrick said, choking on his emotion. "We all are."

Phyre came forward then, and hugged Thairyn. "I knew you would find your gift," she said. "You were so certain you had one, it had to appear sometime. Mother always said, just wait, and it will come. She was right."

Jewl stepped up next. "I'm sorry I was mean to you, Thairyn," Jewl said shyly. "I'm glad you are all right. I'm glad you have a birth-gift like me. Now I don't have to be alone." She hugged him tightly and whispered in his ear, "And I don't have to be crown matriarch either."

*   *   *

While Thairyn was telling his story and answering the many questions his family had for him, Arreshi, captain of the guard, questioned Arth in his cell. As the family returned to the celebration festivities after sunset, the captain reported her findings to Merrick privately.

"He is telling the truth, your highness," remarked Arreshi.

"And their stories seem to match well," commented Merrick.

"But, I advise caution, your highness."

"Well said, Captain. We will be watchful of both Arth and my son for a while yet, lest this be a ruse of some kind."

"I will alert the guards. Shall we keep Arth confined for now?"

"Yes, for now. I have already told him he is to be pardoned, but he has no idea when he will be freed. A few days in a cell should keep him humble and sweating just a bit. After the celebration, if nothing seems amiss, we will release him with a full pardon and commission of honor, but keep him under surveillance for a while longer after he is released."

"Very well, then, your highness."

"Oh, and I will want to have a talk with Arth myself before his release," Merrick added with a smile. "I'm interested in the man who my son called patria. Maybe he can give me some insight."

Arreshi saluted smartly and turned away before she let her smile escape.

Thairyn
visits Arth's
family

Nan Whybant 2018

CHAPTER 28

After two days alone on Claw Island, Naron was slumped on the beach, staring bleakly into the foggy morning light of the third day. His fire had burned down to coals, and he poked at it with a stick, unwilling to get up and fetch more wood. There would be a boat along sometime. There had to be! He cursed Tindus, Arth, and that crown brat for the hundredth time, while he picked a fishbone out of his teeth. He would have to choose more carefully next time, or better yet, just do it himself.

All at once, a triad of dragon riders descended out of the gray mist surrounding him. The riders were quick to capture Naron the kidnapper. While they bound him, Naron blamed Arth and Tindus, and spewed out all he knew about Tindus's last known destination. He laughed when the riders told him they had Arth confined already. Naron watched with satisfaction as one of the dragon riders flew off toward the boat master's dwelling. *I will not suffer alone*, he thought grimly.

Naron cursed his lot again while they strapped him to a dragon saddle, with his hands bound behind him. His stomach lurched when the dragon leapt from the ground, wings pumping to gain altitude. As the two dragons banked left and headed toward en'Edlia, Naron's head spun with the unaccustomed height and movement. His black hordle-tailed hair flew out behind him, and his long, black coat flapped violently in the wind. He continued to struggle against his bonds. He felt he would rather fall to his death than face an eventual trial and prison sentence. The riders had bound him securely and did not allow the kidnapper that chance. They were quick and careful to deliver their catch to justice.

As the heavy, barred door of one of en'Edlia's holding cells closed in his face, Naron swore on his Grandfather Zarcon's head, "I will yet have me revenge!"

*　　*　　*

The day after the Installation of the Ascending Oracle celebration ended, Arth was released with new clothes and his pardon, along with a commission of honor for risking his life to protect and save the heir to the throne of en'Edlia. He was also given a good sum of pa'trees as payment for the information, which led to the capture, or knowledge of the whereabouts of the other kidnappers.

"En'Edlia thanks you for your service, Arth," the high patriarch said formally. Then he winked and whispered, "And thanks for the advice on being a good patria!" Merrick laughed while he clasped the big man's hand.

Arth's face colored with embarrassment, but he smiled. Who would have ever thought he would be giving advice to the high patriarch himself! Arth watched the realm's leader walk away, and then turned to be on his own way. He would return home. It would take several days, even with the hordle and wagon he had acquired and filled with gifts and supplies for his family, but he needed the time to think. The high patriarch had also given him some counsel on keeping wives happy and his small realm running smoothly. Arth knew he had much to make up for as he began the long trip to his small farm on the west side of Serpent's Tongue River.

*   *   *

"Patria! Patria! Patria! Patria!" four children cried. They leaped around their father, dancing and smiling.

"Patria has come home to us!" cried Betheliza excitedly.

"I knew you would!" yelled Chemail. The youngest, Eloreen, just cried as she hugged her older sister, Lanaia.

Arth's eyes filled with shameful tears as he knelt and drew his merciful children into his embrace. It seemed they had all doubled in size since he had last seen them. He loved them all. *Why did I ever leave them?* he thought bitterly.

However, Arth's wife, Ennela, wasn't so forgiving. It was true her eyes had popped when she had seen the sum of pa'trees her husband had in his purse and the documents of pardon and honor, but she was still distrustful. "We will see," she said. "If there is a next time, there will be no pardon from this house, even if you come home a king!"

Arth made sure there never was a next time, for after that he was the most faithful husband and attentive father who ever lived on Irth. His family enjoyed playing and working together, and they especially loved it when Crown Patriarch Thairyn, the best dragon rider on Irth, and Kluus, the ruby dragon, came to visit and play catch-me-if-you-can in the farm's fields.

Printed in the United States
By Bookmasters